the blue
lawn

the blue lawn

by
William Taylor

 alyson books
los angeles | new york

© 1994 BY WILLIAM TAYLOR. ALL RIGHTS RESERVED.

MANUFACTURED IN THE UNITED STATES OF AMERICA.

THIS TRADE PAPERBACK ORIGINAL IS PUBLISHED BY ALYSON PUBLICATIONS,
P.O. BOX 4371, LOS ANGELES, CALIFORNIA 90078-4371.
DISTRIBUTION IN THE UNITED KINGDOM BY TURNAROUND PUBLISHER SERVICES LTD.,
UNIT 3 OLYMPIA TRADING ESTATE, COBURG ROAD, WOOD GREEN,
LONDON N22 6TZ ENGLAND.

FIRST PUBLISHED BY HARPERCOLLINS PUBLISHERS (NEW ZEALAND) LTD.: 1994
SECOND HARPERCOLLINS EDITION: 1995
FIRST ALYSON BOOKS EDITION: MAY 1999

99 00 01 02 03 **a** 10 9 8 7 6 5 4 3 2

ISBN 1-55583-493-0
(PREVIOUSLY PUBLISHED WITH ISBN 1-86950-140-3 BY HARPERCOLLINS PUBLISHERS.)

LIBRARY OF CONGRESS CATALOGING-IN-PUBLICATION DATA
TAYLOR, WILLIAM, 1938–
    THE BLUE LAWN / BY WILLIAM TAYLOR.—1ST ALYSON ED.
    SUMMARY: A FIFTEEN-YEAR-OLD BOY ACKNOWLEDGES HIS ATTRACTION TO AN
OLDER RUGBY TEAMMATE AS HE ALSO BEGINS TO BREAK OUT OF PRECONCEIVED
NOTIONS ABOUT HIM HELD BY HIS FAMILY AND OTHERS.
    ISBN 1-55583-493-0
    [1. HOMOSEXUALITY—FICTION. 2. COMING OF AGE—FICTION. 3. NEW
ZEALAND—FICTION.] I. TITLE.
PZ7.T21875B1 1999   99-11761 CIP
[FIC]—DC21

For Glenda Fulton

1

It had been a hard run. The rain and the wind had driven in at them, needle sharp. The cold was such that the run had been almost over before the exercise had started to warm any of them.

The changing room emptied quickly. No one was interested in a cold shower and most had hastily towelled off heads and faces and had clambered, sticky and half-wet, back into their clothes before taking off into the gathering dusk. There was no talk. In ten minutes only two remained in the dank gloom.

Their coach poked his head around the door. 'Come on you two. Get a move on. I'm off,' and a moment later they heard the sound of his car as it backed from the parking lot outside and then took off.

The one who seemed to be the younger of the two busied himself, stripped from half-sodden shorts and T-shirt, pulled on clothing and wrinkled his face in a grimace of distaste. His clothes resisted, the wool and the cotton reluctant, uncomfortable and prickling against his skin. The discomfort was the least of his worries. His mind, all his attention was directed towards the other and his effort was spent in not betraying this.

The older of the two had not moved during the whole of the short, sharp pantomime of fast change and swift exit. He continued to rest on the bench where he had slumped after coming in from the run. He gave no sign that he noticed the presence of the other. Now, he hooked a toe around his sport bag and drew it, grating, across the concrete floor towards him. He fished in among the jumbled contents. He took out cigarettes, a lighter, lit up and then slumped back again against the wall. He took two or three deep drags, blew a cloud of smoke into the damp air, wrinkled his face and then flicked the unfinished cigarette across the room and into a urinal. He put his arms behind his head, closed his eyes briefly and sighed. Then he stood, stretched and started to strip from his running gear. The movement brought him closer to the other, who had almost finished changing and was busy shoving a ball of wet clothing into his bag. His hand shook slightly as he tugged at a reluctant zip.

The younger one stood, swallowed hard and looked, for the first time directly, at the older.

'Had a good eyeful, kid? Been having one these last ten minutes, eh? What d'you want now? A handful?'

The younger boy jumped, recoiled as if shot. As the other laughed at his discomfort he thrust the last of his gear into his bag and pulled on his jacket. He was hot. Hot and, he knew, flushing red. He moved to the door, head down. The older one stood in the doorway. 'What d'you say? Eh?'

'Get out of my way.' The younger spoke for the first time.

'That what you want?'

Emotion welled in the younger. He swung his bag hard in the direction of his tormentor, who side-stepped neatly, laughing. The bag thunked, clanged uselessly against a bank of lockers. Rage rose, swelled acid into his throat and he flung his bag aside and himself onto the older one.

The meeting was short, sharp, brutal. Physical advantage lay fully with the younger. Knee to groin, one left hook, a right and it was all over. Twenty seconds, less, and the older boy, still half-naked, slid, gasping, down the concrete wall and rested, knees to chin and head and face averted from the attacker standing over him. The younger one caught breath in short and shallow gasps and the muscles of his face worked, twitched, and there was a bewildered look in his eyes. Without taking those eyes from the older he reached for his bag and edged through the door and ran into the wet night.

His mother fussed. 'David, David. You've hardly touched your food, dear. And it's one of your favourites.'

'How'd the training go?' asked his father.

'Pretty cold. Got a bit of a chill, I reckon. Okay if I have an early night?'

'Good idea, love. I'll do you some hot lemon,' said his mother.

'Stop fussing, woman,' said his father.

'It's beyond me why they put you through this nonsense in weather like this. Good Lord, it's only a game,' said his mother.

'Nonsense it might be,' smiled his father. 'But you should just hear what they're saying about this guy and his future down the club. Sky's the limit, they reckon.'

'Doesn't make it any the less a load of nonsense,' said his mother. 'You take off to bed, Davy. I'll just rustle up a nice hot lemon and honey.'

'Put a slug of whisky in it, too. Boy's big enough. Put a few more hairs where they're meant to be,' the father chuckled.

'It's okay. It's okay,' said their son, wishing he had said nothing in the first place. 'Don't want anything. Honest I don't. Reckon all I need's an early night,' and he tried to smile his gratitude through to both of them. 'No more'n a bit tired. I'll have a shower and go to bed.'

'If this wretched weather doesn't clear, you stay home tomorrow, David. One day off school won't hurt you and it's just so foul.'

'Don't coddle the boy, woman. He's a man, not a mouse. A man's game he plays, too. Let him be.'

The son tried to smile. 'It's all right,' he said, in reply, he knew, to nothing. He went to his room.

He took a long shower and stood, letting the needle jets of hot water prick, too hot, into his skin. Usually he used this chance to play, to use every soap, every potion, every shampoo, conditioner and with whatever else his mother stocked the bathroom. He felt numb. He felt as nothing and the water hitting into him increased that feeling of nothingness. Finally he dried and, using a corner of his towel, de-misted the long wall mirror. He combed his hair and looked at his reflection. It was no gaze of self admiration.

He was tall, above average for his age. Well built. Solid, but certainly not fat. Strong neck and broad in the shoulder. Equally strong in leg and arm and well-muscled for his almost sixteen years. Intensely, intently he looked into the mirrored image of his face almost as if he were trying to see further into himself than the mirror would allow. He shook his head as if disappointed that the surface image alone was all he could get. His was a pleasant face. Unremarkable. No great success story. No great disaster. Good eyes, grey. Good crop of fairish and straight hair. All the other normal bits and pieces. He blinked, shook his head back into reality and felt with a finger along the ridge of his chin. Good. No need to shave. As yet, once a week was often enough.

Then he stood back from the mirror and took in the whole of himself in an almost puzzled examining of what he saw. He closed his eyes, bit his lip, swayed slightly for a moment or two and opened his eyes again for another look. He looked very closely. Nothing different. There was nothing different at all from what he considered should be there or from what, he thought, might be the norm.

Quickly he tidied the bathroom, pulled on his bathrobe and went through to his bedroom. He did not go to bed but lay on the patchwork spread, thinking.

He heard the phone ring out in the hall and his mother's voice mingle with the sounds of the television coming through the open door of the room behind her. A knock on his door, and 'Still awake, Davy?'

'Yeah,' he called back.

She came in. 'Not asleep and not quite in bed, either,' she smiled. 'One of your friends, I think. Says it's important. I said it could wait . . .'

'It's okay, Mum. I'm all right. I'll take it.'

'You sure?'

'I'm fine, Mum. Really,' he smiled at her.

'Look, I'll just tell him . . .'

'Leave it, Mother. I'll take it. No big deal,' he pulled himself up from the bed. 'I'm good as gold. It was just the wet and cold earlier. That's all.'

'If you say so. Now you just stay there. I'll bring the phone. Plug it in here. Time we got one for your room.'

5

'Yeah,' he said into the phone and waited, expecting the voice of one of his friends.

Nothing.

'Are you there?' and he was about to hang up. Then he heard a soft breathing and he knew. He felt himself hot again. Hot. Hot and ashamed. He pulled the collar of his robe away from his neck and at the same time felt the pulse throbbing in his throat.

'I just called to apologise. To say sorry.' The voice was very soft.

David mouthed, but no sound came. He wet his lips with his tongue and sighed. He put down the receiver without a word. He leaned back against the headboard of his bed, eyed the phone, apprehensive. It was almost as if he expected the appliance itself to talk back at him. Then it rang again. He knew who it would be and picked up the receiver quickly.

'Hey. It's okay,' said the voice. 'I'm sorry. Don't you worry.'

This time he managed to speak and he knew his voice was strained, edgily high. 'Was me hit you. Was me hit you and you're sorry?'

'Face it, kid. Anyone'd be sorry to be hit like that. But, hell, I asked for it.'

David spoke slowly. 'Never hit no one like that before. Not like that. Not ever.'

'Shit, kid. Coulda fooled me.'

'I never . . . I just never done that. Not since for as long as I can remember.'

'Yeah. So, I believe you. Might be as well you don't get used to it. Fists and knees of yours could sort of be called deadly weapons. Can still feel the effect and that's for sure. Reckon you just might've done me some permanent damage.'

6

'I . . . er . . .' A croak.

'It's okay, kid. Don't worry.'

'I . . . I don't know what made me do it.'

'Huh? Don't you?' asked the voice. A pause and then a short laugh. 'No, reckon maybe you don't at that.'

'What do you mean?'

'I don't mean anything, kid. Nothing at all. No hidden meanings. No hard feelings?'

'Eh?'

'Look. It's Friday tomorrow and I'm away. Won't be at school. How about Saturday you come round here, my place, say hello. How about it?'

'You . . . you mean that?' David breathed deeply.

'Well,' said the other. 'Just might be easier talking to you face-to-face than over the bloody phone. You sure are one dead loss on the phone. Know where I live?'

'Yeah. Yeah, I do.' Too quick.

'Make it afternoon, then. Now get back to bed, kid.'

'How did you know I was in bed?'

'Know everything, kid. Don't you forget it. Sweet dreams.' The short laugh again. 'Or whatever else you fancy,' and the receiver at the other end clicked down.

David got off his bed and pulled back the covers as if to get in. He changed his mind and went back out to the livingroom. 'Feel fine now, Mum,' he said.

'Who was that on the phone, dear? Didn't recognise the voice and he didn't say.'

'No one, Mum. No one at all. Just one of the guys.'

'Come here,' she ordered.

He went to her and she felt his forehead. 'Hmm. Yes. No temperature, anyway. Still, might be an idea if you do take the day off.'

'God, woman. Stop mollycoddling the boy.' His father smiled at them both. 'How about we all have a nice cup of tea?'

'Sounds fine by me,' said his wife. 'Seeing as how you're offering to make it.'

'Wasn't exactly thinking of going that far,' he said.

'No. I didn't think you were,' she laughed.

'Sit down, Mum. I'll get it,' said their son.

2

David Mason took his mother's advice and stayed home. The Friday was as cold, wet and windy as the day before and it took little extra persuasion. He said no to her offer of breakfast in bed and said he'd get up, mid-morning, and get something for himself. 'You're not to go outside,' she said. 'Just wouldn't surprise me at all if you were coming down with something or other,' and she fussed about his room and about him.

'Nothing wrong that a day in bed won't fix,' and he tried what he hoped was a small and sickly smile at her. Ill-health was not something he knew much about. His mother kissed him and left.

Jack Mason, his father, had already left the house. It was stocktaking time at the hardware store Jack had owned and operated for the twenty-five years the family had lived in the town. David heard his mother's car pull out of the garage and she, too, was gone. For a dozen years, now, Maureen Mason had taught a class of seven-year-olds at the local primary school where, once, David had been a pupil.

David yawned, stretched and then snuggled back into the welcome warmth of his bed. Maxwell, the family cat, joined him and they both snoozed on into the morning.

He got up at eleven, dressed and went through to the kitchen and ate four cold sausages from the fridge, opened and ate most of the contents of a can of spaghetti, cold, toasted and consumed several pieces of toast and made his way through half a packet of chocolate biscuits with the help of a cup of coffee. 'Feed a cold and starve a fever,' he muttered to himself. 'Or does Mum say it the other way round?' He shrugged. 'What the hell?' It was still not midday and the day stretched too far in front of him. Turned on the telly. Turned it off, sat on the hearth, drank another cup of coffee. Maxwell the cat, deprived of warmth in one haven, tracked it down to another and stretched his ginger length in front of the heater and went back to sleep. 'God. You sure got one great life,' said David to the cat. 'Not a care in the whole bloody world.' He nudged the animal with his toe.

He wandered the room restlessly, stopping, standing for a moment and gazing unseeingly through the rain-streaked sittingroom window into the desolation of the late-autumn, wind-battered garden beyond. He made himself a third cup of coffee and sat in an armchair, sipping, staring vacantly at the dead screen of the television. He did not need his thinking to stray or wander into thought of the other. It was as if that other were there with him, not only at this moment but at all waking moments. Right there, in his head, with him. Had been there a moment ago, was there right now, would be there a moment hence. Now, of course, there was the feel of him, too. The feel of his own knuckles when, on the night before, they had hit into smooth flesh.

Then there was the seeing of him. Seeing him back through every school day for months now. The occasional sighting away from school. Seeing him as he sat in class, three rows in front, one across and over by the wall against which, idle, he would lean back, lounging, lazing, taking all in. See, too, the set of him, the tight-legged, washed-out jeans none of them was supposed to wear, the softness of the sweaters, blue, red, grey, that again he wore in careless disregard of any regulation. The deep dark brown hair, short, with one, lazy, blonded curl in front like some sort of pale question mark. Something gold, lizard-life about the whole of him. The taut, tight, olive skin and the high cheek bones that he, David, had hit. Eyes, pale and compelling, a surprising light blue, slanted into an otherwise dark face. Eyes that mocked. Eyes that said they saw everything and knew too much.

Foreign in every way. Especially in these parts. An outsider, an alien from God knew where. Theo. Theodore Meyer. Said nothing about himself, nothing of where he had come from, why he had come or how long he was going to stay. Pushed off, parried off the thrust of any questions. A skilful fencer. An outsider happy to be outside, happy to set himself apart and to stay apart. He drove his own car. Small, fast, red and Japanese. He arrived as the first school bell sounded, left during lunch breaks and took off again after school as soon as he could. Foreign in every way. An outsider. A stranger.

'Wanna cup of coffee, Max?' David sighed, stroked the cat with a toe. 'Like a cuppa? No? Want a mouse, eh? A big, fat, juicy, fresh-live mouse?' He stroked some more. 'Well, mate, you're tough outa luck unless you go get one for yourself.' David got up, wandered through to the kitchen, made an effort to wash a few dishes, made another cup of coffee and settled into the second half of the packet of chocolate biscuits and a talk-show on television. Although his eyes were on the screen he took in little. He was still sitting there when his mother got home.

'Okay, love?' She kissed him on the head and ruffled his hair. 'Dear God, they were demons today. I know it's the weather, but . . . How d'you feel?'

'Fine, Mum,' he smiled at her. 'Just been taking it easy like you said. Even managed a bit of food, eh. You sit down and I'll get you a coffee.'

'There's a packet of chocolate biscuits I got in yesterday. Could sure do with a bit of an energy buzz. They're on top of the cake tin, love,' she called through to him.

'Can't spot them, Mum,' he called back.

'I'm not surprised,' said his mother, smiling. 'Looks as though Maxwell ate them all. Must've dragged the packet into here.'

'Yeah, Mum. I remember. He did. I tried to stop him.' David handed his mother her drink.

Maureen Mason looked at her son over the rim of her coffee mug as she blew onto the scalding liquid. 'What's on your mind, Davy?'

'What d'you mean?' he asked, defensive.

'Don't play games with me, young man,' she said. 'Spit it out.'

'It's . . . it's nothing,' he said.

She sighed. 'I've lived long enough to know that when someone says it's nothing it's generally something. Come on. Tell me.'

'You're not going to like it. Dad even less.'

She looked at the worried frown on his face and sat, silent and still for a while. 'David,' she started. 'I can't even begin to imagine what it is and I can't begin to imagine that it's not something that can't be fixed or

12

talked through. I've only got one son and from what I see, what I hear, what I know, your father and me are pretty damn' lucky with the one we've got. You'll do us, warts and all. Look at your Dad, now, prouder'n any peacock at you and what you do, most particularly on the wretched rugby field, I might add. Your ability there is the talk of not only your school and his club but of half the district as well. I . . .'

David interrupted, 'Yeah. That's it. If you must know, that's it.'

'What d'you mean?'

'Bloody rugby. That's it.' David looked grimly at her.

'Tell me?' she asked, quietly.

'I want to give it away. That's what,' said her son.

'Whew. So that's it,' she said, softly.

'And that sure won't go down easy. See what I mean?'

'Why?' she asked.

He looked around the room as if to get some help in what he had to say. The warm and familiar ordinariness of the place was of some small comfort. He groped for the right words. 'I don't think you'd understand. I know Dad won't. I don't want to hurt you and I don't want to hurt him.'

'So?'

'I've felt this way for a long time. I . . . I want to give it away and . . .'

'And what?'

'Well, I couldn't. Not really. Last two years, you know, I've come to hate it. And I hate me doing it. Beginning of the season's worse, worst . . . then, when things get going I just sort of, like, put it on a back burner and put up with it and it all ends up not quite as bad.'

'But not quite as bad isn't good enough any more? Is that what you mean?' his mother asked.

13

David sighed. 'Yeah. Guess it's something like that. But I've decided now I'm not going to go on. I don't like it and I don't want it. It's . . . it's . . .' He struggled for more words. 'It's as if it has taken me over. Taken me over as a person and I've become some sort of machine and it's my only reason for, well, sort of existing and being. It's as if it's the only thing that makes me any-thing to anyone. And the only thing that makes me anything is that I'm good with a bloody rugby ball.'

'You've put that quite well,' said his mother.

'So? You sound surprised.' He managed a slight smile. 'That's not all there is. See . . . I'm me. I'm Dave Mason. I'm not just some guy, some clown who can pick up a bloody ball and run.' He rubbed at his eyes with the back of a hand. 'I said enough. Said it all wrong, I reckon. Don't think I hate the game. Don't think you can really hate something you do quite well. Don't know. Just I don't want to be part of it for a while. I know what I don't like and that's me being some little-time star of what it all is and people seeing me as just that and only that. Gotta get out, Mum. Least for a while.'

'All this time and you never let on. Were Dad and me so blind?'

He looked at her for a moment. 'Yes. Yes, Mum. I think you were. Dad probably more'n you.'

Maureen Mason raised her eyebrows. 'You're not let-ting us off lightly, are you?'

'You asked to know. I can't say any different once I start to tell it.'

'No. Of course you can't,' she said. 'God knows how you'll tell your father. He's so all-fire proud of you.'

'Guess that's all part of it,' said David. 'I don't feel too hot about having to tell him. And you're not to say anything. This is one thing I gotta do. Don't you dare say anything. Promise?'

'I promise,' she sighed. 'Well, your blessed duck hunting and shooting opens in a week or so. Maybe the full fire and heat of that'll give you the moment . . .' She looked at him very hard. 'Dear God! Not that, too?'

He laughed. 'Don't you worry your old grey head. I'll give the old guy another season or two of that before I hang up me gun.' He gave another short laugh. 'Wanna know something?'

'No, no.' She held up a hand. 'You've given me more than enough for one day.'

'Well, it was a toss-up which it'd be first. The rugby or the ducks. Reckon the ducks lost.' He looked at her. 'I love my Dad,' he said, simply.

'I know you do, Davy. We both love you.'

'It's just . . . well, I can't go on for ever doing things and being something that I'm not. You know that. You understand?'

'I understand,' she said, sighing again. 'I think you're telling me you're growing up. I think you're telling me I might have been a bit blind to what all that means. I think you're telling me you're your own man. Quite right, too.'

'You're okay, Mum,' he said, and, standing, walked to her chair and bent to kiss her.

'Gee,' she said. 'Thanks for the vote of confidence. Now you can give the poor old girl a hand with dinner. Your Dad'll be in shortly and I know he wants to get back down to the store to do a bit more on his stocktake. I take it you've no more surprises up your sleeve for me at this sitting?'

He looked down a her. Looked away. Walked to the window and looked out. 'No,' he said. 'No, I haven't,' and he bit very hard on his bottom lip.

15

3

David knew where the house was. The town was small and it was everyone's business when the woman moved in. She had lived in a motel for six months and had daily superintended the building of her home and initial layout of its grounds and garden. New houses were a novelty in these parts and the reasons for her arrival were the subject of much gossip. Sometimes, but not often, she would be seen around the town. She spoke, smiled and was pleasant, but gave nothing of herself.

Everyone knew, too, when at the beginning of this year, her grandson had joined her. Not that his arrival added much to the sum total of town knowledge of the situation. He spoke, smiled, was pleasant but also gave nothing.

The house lay beyond the town and at the end of a driveway that wound down a small rise to where the dwelling was sited, nestled into a slight hollow. Long and low it lay to the sun. It snuggled into its hillside and gardens swept from the terraced house-front, eighty metres or more to a pond, a miniature lake that had been achieved by damming a trickle of stream. The building was beautiful. So too, in time, would be the grounds.

16

David paused for a moment to more fully take in the sight. White house, green hollow and a sweep of gravelled, red cobblestoned driveway and yard. He spotted no sign of life. However, the red Mazda was parked in one bay of the double garage and he guessed Theo was around somewhere. As he crunched across the gravel of the drive the door opened and Theo stood there. 'You came.' It wasn't quite a question.

'Hi.'

'You didn't walk?'

'Not that far.'

The jewelled quality of the place carried through to the inside. It was not a large house. The living, eating and kitchen area was one. Two or three rooms opened off beyond this. Both very simple and very complex. The whole of the interior was a soft almost-white. Heavy velvet drapes hung at all windows. Deep, deep blue curtaining. Scattered across the polished floorboards was a collection of rugs, a multi-coloured rainbow in vivid contrast to the plain surrounds. The furniture was simple. Windows looked out onto the expanse of garden and down to the pond.

'Wanna drink?'

'Yeah. Thanks.'

Theo walked across the room to a cupboard. 'Jim Beam? Southern Comfort? Name your poison,' he laughed. 'Just joking,' he added.

David was not so sure. 'Coke,' he said.

Theo walked to the kitchen fridge and got out two cans, tossed one to David and opened his own. 'You're allowed to sit down,' he said.

David wondered why he had come, took a long swig of his drink and felt uneasy. The whole place, the whole situation was too alien. Just so different from the warm and ordinary comfort he knew. His discomfort was made no less by this other one who sat, half-smiling, staring at him through those slitted pale eyes. Waiting. Waiting for what? David cleared his throat. 'Nice place you got here,' he said.

Theo lit a cigarette. 'Want one?' he extended the pack.

'I don't smoke.'

'Of course not. Care for something a bit stronger in your Coke?'

'No. No thanks.'

'You don't drink, either?'

'Yeah. Yeah, I do. I have a beer sometimes.'

'Wow!' said Theo, and he laughed. 'It's okay, kid. I'm just having you on. I don't drink, either. Well, not much. Well, just sometimes.'

'You sure smoke,' said David.

'Yep.'

'Why?'

'Because I want to.'

There seemed nothing more to say. They sat in silence. David drank from his can, conscious of the noise of the gurgle and gulp of the action. Equally conscious that all the while his host did not take his eyes from him. Unease built. He shouldn't have come here. 'Where's your . . .?'

'Getting a load of sheep shit for her garden. She'll be in soon. She's out at some farm with a sheep shit mine. I was gonna help but I remembered you might come.'

'You could've left a note on the door,' said David.

'That wouldn't have been very nice,' said Theo.

'Does she like living here?' David asked.

'You'll have to ask her, won't you?'

'Do you like living here?'

'No.'

'Why're you here?'

Theo stubbed out his cigarette. 'Not much option. That's why. I live with my mother. She's in Europe for a year. She's a journalist.'

'You could've gone.'

'Yeah. I could've. I nearly did. Always have before. But I need a couple of years at the same school. You know, get those bits of paper which say you've passed things. Wasn't going to get none of those if I tagged along with Mummy yet again. Grandmama was the only answer.'

'Grandmama was the only answer to what?'

Neither boy had heard her come in. 'The answer to my prayers, old lady,' said Theo.

'It gives me a shiver up and down my spine to think what the answer to any prayer of yours might be, Theodore,' the woman laughed. 'I left the car down the driveway by the spot where I want the manure. Perhaps you and your friend would unload it for me. I am so, so sorry, Theo. Please introduce me.'

Theo stood. 'Gretel, this is David Mason. We're in the same class at school. David, this is my grandmother, Gretel Meyer.' He spoke formally, correctly.

'The boy from the hardware store. Right?'

'How d'you do, Mrs Meyer.'

'It's Gretel.'

David swallowed. First name terms with his elders was beyond his experience. Safer to settle for nothing.

'Lump those sacks, Theo, and give me a chance to change.' She said her grandson's name with a hard 'T'. 'Then I can entertain and show our guest a little better respect.'

They heaved sacks and David wondered why anyone who could afford a Porsche needed to dig, bag and spread her own sheep droppings. Surely Porsche owners had whole teams of gardeners? And surely this was the only Porsche owner, ever, to make room for a couple of sacks of sheep manure on the front passenger seat of her car!

They finished and went back inside. Gretel Meyer, washed and changed, was making coffee. A tiny woman. Slight, very thin and no taller than his, David's shoulder. Straight, steel-grey hair pulled back from the face and knotted at the neck. Sharp featured and with piercing eyes that were almost black. There was little difference in the way grandmother or grandson dressed. She wore a loose, woollen sweater and tight jeans. Gretel Meyer could have been fifty. She could have been seventy. She spoke clearly, precisely and with an accent that said she had probably been born elsewhere.

'Coffee? Of course,' she answered herself. 'Now, David Mason from the hardware store. You tell me about yourself.'

Theo confused David. So, too, did Theo's grandmother. 'Tell . . . tell you what?'

'Well, boy, what do you do and where do you live and what do you do with yourself and all of that?' She gave a little bark of a laugh. 'But, see, I think I know all that.'

'You do?'

Theo leaned back in his chair, an amused eye on his guest. He was smoking again and it surprised David that the grandmother said nothing. He thought of his own grandmothers. They were nothing like Gretel Meyer.

'I course I know,' said Gretel. 'I read every word in your local, our local newspaper. It doesn't take long.' She barked another small laugh. 'You are the big star football player with the great future. I know that much. And my grandson tells me you are in the same class at school. I know that. I have seen your father's shop and I imagine because it has "Mason" written up over the door it must belong to him. And I do believe your mother is a nurse. No? A teacher? Right?'

'Whew,' said David.

'Grandmama thinks she is a great detective,' said Theo.

'Grandmama knows she is a great big fool,' said Gretel. 'Why else would she have her great big grandson living with her and eating her out of house and home and not doing a hand's stitch?'

'A hand's turn,' said Theo.

'I know what I mean,' said Gretel. She turned back to David. 'And you have that lovely garden and the old house just on the outside of town. I've thought to ask to see it some time.'

'I think it is nowhere near as good as your garden will be, Mrs Meyer . . . er, Gretel. Your garden will soon be very good. I would like to have a good look round it if you would let me,' said David.

'Christ! Not another gardener,' said Theo.

'Aha!' Gretel Meyer clapped her hands. 'Aha!' she said again. 'I know the moment I saw you, Mr Football Star, there is more to you . . .'

'What do you mean?' David was more confused than ever. What had he said?

'This is a friend you can keep, Theodore. You don't disappoint me, David Mason. You ask about the garden, eh? You don't ask about the car. I like it.' She smiled at him.

Suddenly David felt more at ease. He smiled at Gretel. 'I like gardens,' he said. 'Very much indeed. I think growing things is pretty good. Watching them grow and all that. And I sure like cars, too. I was going to ask you about your one. Just that you happened to mention the garden before I got a chance.'

'This Theo, here, he couldn't tell a rose from a rag-wort. Useless to talk to. Useless to get to work. One day he thought he helped me and burnt up three, four shrubs because they had lost their leaves. Thought they looked dead,' said Gretel.

'They sure are now,' said Theo.

'Yes, my boy. I tell you if I had been around then, so would you have been,' said his grandmother.

'That's gratitude for you.' Theo shook his head.

'So, you like gardens?' she snapped at David again.

'We sell trees and shrubs and plants at the shop,' he said.

'I know. I buy them. Some of my things are from your shop.'

'We don't have very much,' said David.

'I know,' she said.

'See, I want to leave school and work on that part of our business. It's the part of what Dad does that really interests me,' said David.

'Is good,' said Gretel. 'But you stay at school first. Then you go study horticulture and gardening. Then you really know something about it.'

'Yeah. I know that.' He grinned at her. 'That's what Mum and Dad say I gotta do. But I could leave. Just on old enough to leave.'

'So . . . o.' She drew out the word. 'So, we're grown up, are we?' Gretel Meyer lit a cigarette.

The smoke was foul and David, without thinking, must have shown distaste. He coughed slightly.

'Hah, boy! I'll open a window. You come here you

22

must put up with this.' She waved her cigarette. 'Big big vice. They are French I smoke.'

Theo laughed at David. 'See. It's all her fault. Me? I gotta smoke in self defence.'

'What nonsense,' said Gretal Meyer, and turned to David. 'You come again to see me.' She finished her coffee. 'You come again to see me and we walk round the garden and you can give me — what do they call it? — yes, the benefit of your local knowledge.'

'I'm not that good. Don't know too much,' said David.

'No matter. We learn together, you and I. I know nearly nothing at all. The more I learn the less I seem to know. Good day, young man.' She left the room.'

'Old girl likes you. Gardening, eh? Gardening? Me? I don't know squat.' Theo looked at David. 'She doesn't like many people.'

'She's . . . she's . . .'

'She's what?'

'A pretty interesting lady,' said David.

'Yeah, I reckon,' said Theo. 'Come on. We'll go out to my room.' He stood.

Theo's room was at the back of the garage. Self-contained. Plain, almost bare. A bed, a dresser, a rug on the floor, a table and a chair. Almost a cell. A doorway led through to a small bathroom and shower.

'Great,' said David. 'Shit! I'd give my eye teeth for a place like this. You could do what you like in a place like this and no one'd ever know.'

'I do,' said Theo.

'Do what?' puzzled.

'What I like out here.' A smile. 'Sit down. Use the bed if you like.' He lit another cigarette.

'God. You smoke a helluva lot,' said David.

'Look, kid. I do what I do. You do what you do. Get

23

off my . . .'

'I didn't mean . . .' David began.

'Yes, you did,' said Theo, blowing a cloud of smoke in David's direction. He sat down on the bottom of the bed. 'Mind you, kid, I could sure criticise you for one or two things you do quite well that are even more anti-social.' He rubbed his chin.

'You asked for that,' said David.

'Yeah. Tell me about it,' and Theo laughed. 'Tell me about yourself, kid.'

David laughed back at him. 'Tell you about me? Nothing to tell. You can't want to know about me. Look at you. Look at your granny. Look at all this,' he gestured. 'That car out there. You tell me about you and then tell me about her and then tell me about that car.'

'Ho, ho. So it wasn't the garden, eh? It is the car? Aw, think I'd better go and tell Granny.'

'You can tell what you like.'

'It's just a Porsche. Okay, so they don't grow on trees but they aren't that uncommon. It's only money . . .'

'But an er . . . old er . . .'

'Lady driving one? Sure. Why not? She can afford it. She likes it. Why not? It's like me smoking,' said Theo.

'Nothing like,' said David.

'No. You tell me about you. You know. A day in the life of a hick-town hunk. What makes the little hick tick?'

David stood. 'Shit on you,' he said, and turned to walk out the door.

'Hey, kid. Sorry.' He raised a hand in mock defence. 'Don't hit me again. Please. Please don't hit me again. I might grow to like it.'

David stopped just short of the door, turned and walked to look out of the small window. Part of him wanted to leave. Badly. Part of him wanted to get out of this little, stuffy, smokey room and away from the face, the face, the eyes, the body sprawling on the bed. But he couldn't. Everything in that little room acted as if it were a magnet.

'You're right, kid.' Theo sat up. 'I am a shit.' He spoke softly. 'I am sorry. I mean that.'

'Dunno what made me come here,' David muttered.

'Don't you?' asked Theo.

'I'll tell you about me,' he said, simply. 'Lived here for ever. You know about the store we got. Got a sister as well as Mum and Dad. Janet. Lives in Auckland. She's a nurse. Older'n me by about nine years. Don't see her often. What else? Oh, yeah. I go to school. You know that. I'm okay, but not all that shit hot. Got a lot of mates. Sort of known them all for as long as I can remember. I want to do a polytech course in plants and gardens. In a few weeks I'll be sixteen but I'm bigger'n most guys my age and don't ask me which bits are bigger,' and he smiled. 'Okay?'

'Nope,' said Theo. 'But guess it's a start. I could've told you most of that about you from what little I know already. See, it's like this. I want to know what you think. I want to know where you're at. I want to know what makes you happy and, then, what scares you shitless. I want to know, too, if you get your kicks, get a buzz from those two girls you work with all the time in the science lab who don't know a damn thing about chemistry but who stick to you like glue . . .'

'What a loada crap,' said David. 'And Julie's my cousin.

'I don't care if she's your aunty. She gets off, big time, standing close to you and both staring in the same test-tube,' said Theo.

'How come you seen all this?'

'That's for me to know,' said Theo. 'Tell me what it's like to be a golden boy sport wonder. God, kid. You could shoot the mayor and they'd give you a medal.'

David laughed. 'Yeah, for doing a public service.' He sat, saying nothing for a moment.

'Yeah, yeah, yeah. You can tell me,' said Theo. 'It's not all a bed of old roses, is it kid?'

'I . . . er . . .'

Theo went on. 'I been keeping an eye on you. Don't worry.' He raised a hand. 'I kept an eye on others, too. Maybe a bit more of one on you, though. After all, it's not as if you haven't been keeping one on me, kid.'

'Do you think you could stop calling me kid?' asked David. 'Pisses me off.'

'Doubt it,' said Theo. 'Even call Grandmama kid.' He looked at David. 'I just reckon from what I seen that it's not all sweetness, light and sugar up on top of your dung heap. I'm right?'

'I'm giving rugby away,' said David. 'That the sort of thing you want to know?'

Theo whistled. 'My word! That's sure to put a pussycat among the little sparrows. So . . . o.' He drew out the word in the manner of his grandmother. 'Daddy has a shop, Mummy is a teacher, the world is my oyster but I'm getting sick of the shell.'

David spoke slowly. 'I'm not too sure of what I'm doing or even why I want to do it. I know it'll half kill my dad and at school I think my name will be slime for some long time.'

'Aw. Poor little fella. Don't feel sorry for yourself. Give up the physical jerk crap and you can take up smoking,' said Theo.

'You reckon?' David laughed. 'It's just I don't want

to hurt any of them.'

'Jesus, kid! Of course you'll hurt them. That's part of the game. But, you go on and you don't want to . . . who ends up hurt then? Look at it. You're piggy in the middle. All the rest of the runts are looking in from the outside, through the fence. Their hurts will be secondhand hurts. Yours is firsthand. Get it?'

'Not really,' said David.

'What'll you do instead?'

'Dunno.'

'You're too nice, kid. Face it. You're too good to be true. Little goody football boots. Your old man'll survive. Guess he means quite a bit to you,' said Theo.

'He does. Guess it'd finish him off good and proper if I told him I was also thinking of giving up duck shooting with him.'

Theo sat up quickly. 'You? You shoot ducks?'

'Yeah,' said David, surprised. 'Heaps of guys do.'

'Holy cow! This I must see. You're telling me you mercilessly slaughter poor defenceless little birds? You? I don't believe I'm hearing this.' Flatly. 'Little goody football boots a violent killer. God!'

'I'm sorry.' David did not know what else to say.

'You're sorry? You're sorry? What about the ducks? What about the poor fucked ducks? Bet they're sorrier.'

'They do get eaten,' said David.

'Must be a big consolation to them,' said Theo. 'Redneck. Hick. Murderer. You violent little redneck. Can I come, too?'

'I guess. It doesn't sound as if you quite approve,' said David.

'Approve? Approve? I think it's bloody great,' said Theo. 'I knew there was some reason for me being here apart from bloody school. Me? I gotta deep feeling I'm a born killer. It's just I can't believe it of quiet, gentle — apart from on the field of rugby, that is — little you, innocent face and all . . . Nah. Can't imagine it.'

'It is a sport,' said David.

'Yeah. Tell that to the ducks. When is it?'

'Coupla weeks.'

'I'll be there. What do I need?'

'Can you shoot?' asked David.

'Well, dunno, do I? Can't be that much to it. Like, it's the guys have the guns. Not the ducks. Piece of cake,' said Theo.

'We'll see,' said David, for the first time that afternoon feeling superior to the other. 'I'm going now.'

Theo stood. 'Come again, kid. Whenever.'

David moved past Theo. Their bodies touched, brushed slightly in the passing. Their eyes caught. Quickly, each looked away from the other.

'I'll run you home in my car,' said Theo.

'I'll walk. Thanks.'

'Sounds like you don't trust my driving,' said Theo.

'Nah. Sounds as if I want to walk,' said David.

'Sounds as if you might be learning,' said Theo. 'You let me know about those ducks. Don't you forget, killer.'

4

When he was with him, when he could see him, talk to him and be with him, it was fine. It was as if everything was normal and was right. It was another thing again when he was at home with his parents or alone — hardest at night before sleep came, when thought niggles, gnaws, corrodes and the cancer sets up a dull and empty ache.

Hard, too, to keep the surface normal with the ripples on the pond shelling out as they should. How not to phone, eager or too often. How to ignore it at school. How to look, but make it look that the eyes looked elsewhere. How to pretend.

Dealing, too, with the everyday problems of everyday living. David spoke to his rugby coach. 'Just for this season, Mr Green. Just gotta have a break so I can work out where I'm going. Don't suppose you'll understand,' and it all proved easier than he had thought.

'Won't pretend it isn't a blow, Davy. Won't pretend I hadn't seen it coming. Got a feeling it's a case of too much too soon and the blame for that rests as much with me as with you. Bit of a bugger, all the same. Wish you'd told me a couple of months back.'

It was as if one of the iron bands constricting David's

gut had snapped and, all of a sudden, movement was easier. 'It's just . . .'

'Don't go on, Davy.' The coach held up a hand. 'Course I want the best for the team. Worked bloody hard for years and this year . . . Still, it's not going to be at the expense of you or anyone else.' He managed a grin at the boy. 'Good as you are, you're not the only pebble on the beach. Have you had a chat to your old man? No? Didn't think you had. Might find him a tougher nut. You're his pride and joy, son.'

Having told the one he could certainly waste no time telling the other. Small town grapevines are fast and efficient.

'What? Not training tonight, boy?' his father asked. 'That coach of yours slacking off some. Didn't spot him at the club tonight and he's generally there if he's not out with you boys.'

'Yeah, Dad. I think there's training,' said David.

'You so good they're giving you a break?' his father chuckled. 'Reckon you'll show 'em all this year. God, only last week it was, down the club, old Nobby Clark saying give it no more'n three years, four maybe, and he'd eat his hat if you're not playing provincial and sky's the limit after that.'

'It's no good, Dad. No easy way of saying this. But I'm giving it away. The rugby. Least for now I am,' said David.

'You are what?' His father stood.

'I don't want to play any more,' said David. His heart thumped. He breathed deeply. Not often had he felt this miserable. 'I just . . . just . . .don't wanna play.' He half-prayed, half-hoped for a response of anger in his father. A loud blast would make it easier. A loud roar would be easier countered. It didn't quite come.

30

'You're a bloody idiot. Right little idiot.' His father sat back down. 'You've got a gift. Now you're chucking it.' He shook his head. 'I don't understand.'

'Reckon I don't, either, Dad. Well not fully,' said his son. 'All I know is that for now I gotta do it this way.' He looked at his father and he didn't like what he saw. The man sat, slumped, in his armchair and it looked to David as if some light had been turned off in his face.

'I just don't understand,' his father repeated. 'You . . . you've got it all. Well, you had it all.'

'So what?' said David. 'You never had to do it, Dad. Never had to go through all the crap. Well, I did. You know what?'

'Go on,' muttered his father. 'Surprise me.'

'Well . . .' David groped for words. 'I might've done it. I just might have it all or whatever. But, you know, none of what I was doing . . . well, I wasn't doing it for me. I never had the guts to say. Not till now.'

His father looked at him and sat in silence for a long while. Then he shrugged, gave a short and mirthless laugh. 'Maybe you're right, boy. I suppose it has taken you a heap of guts to tell me. Still, there's always another year . . .'

'See, Dad, there's other things I want . . .' but he thought better of wandering off the one path, at least for now. 'Yeah, there's always another year, Dad. And I am sorry. Really am.'

'You got nothing to be sorry about, son. I just hope for your sake that you don't have second thoughts some six or seven weeks down the track. Be a bit late by then for you to change your mind. Least for this season.'

'I don't think I'll change my mind, Dad.' He gave a tight little grin. 'Reckon it'll serve me right if I do, eh?'

'Serve you right for what?' His mother came into the room. She looked at her husband and guessed what had gone on. 'He told you then?'

'You knew?'

'He told me last week. The day he was home, sick.' She walked toward David. 'I think it might be the hardest thing he's ever had to tell you, Jack. He knows how much it has meant to you.'

'Stuff 'n nonsense,' said his father, standing. 'Reckon we can do with a drink. All I ever want for the boy is what's best for him. God! Does it really seem to you both that all I been doing is some sort of living my life through him? Load of bull. Come on, boy. Get us a beer, or whatever else your mother might want.'

'His mother can cope with a beer. Sounds good,' said Maureen Mason.

'Anyway,' said his father. 'Week and a bit and those damn ducks'll sure be flying. Reckon that's one thing you'll never be giving up. Right, Davy?'

The mother looked sharply at the son. 'Too right, Dad. God, there's thousands this year. Should see 'em all out on that dam on the north road. Can't wait,' said David.

'We'd better get out to the farm one night this week. Check everything's ready.'

'No sweat, Dad. Whatever,' said David.

The red car drew to a stop beside him. 'Get in, kid. I'll give you a lift. Reminds me. You hear the one about the one-eyed, one-legged, one-armed hitch-hiker? What'd the guy say who stopped for him?'

'Heard it,' said David, tossing his stuff into the back seat and getting in beside Theo. 'Eye eye eye. Hop in.

You look 'armless enough. And it's not one-eyed. It's three-eyed.'

'Bugger you,' said Theo. 'Wish I hadn't stopped.'

'What d'you need to play rugby?'

'Tell me,' said Theo.

'Leather balls,' said David.

'Okay. Let's get onto the real dirty ones,' said Theo. 'You start.'

It was a week since David had visited the Meyer house. Most days, at school, he had seen Theo, but there had been no contact.

'I thought you might have been out to see me . . . us,' said Theo. 'I did say.'

'I didn't like to just call in,' said David. How could he say that this was the one thing, the only thing that he had wanted to do?

'It's up to you, kid. Let's go for a hoon. We'll drive up into those hills over there.' He nodded ahead of him.

'Can I dump my gear at home and change?' David asked. 'I better leave a note. Tell 'em where I've gone.'

Theo smiled. 'Who's a good boy, then? Yeah. Yeah, of course. Nice place you got,' he said, as he pulled into the drive of the Mason home.

It was an old house. Jack and Maureen Mason had done their best to restore it to its late-Victorian state. A high-gabled villa complete with all the latticed, fret-work icing of the period and painted in shades of grey, very pale through to dark. It sat, well set-off, in an expanse of lawn and fringed with the large old trees planted by the original owners of the house. 'I like old houses,' said Theo.

'Well, you can come and have a look inside our one,' said David. 'Wanna drink?'

'Not too long a look,' said Theo. 'Only a couple of

hours before dark. Yeah. I would like to have a look,' and he wandered the house as David changed. 'And we'll take those drinks with us,' he called out. 'Drink and drive, eh? Okay. Okay. Only kidding. Make 'em as soft as you like.'

No cruising. Theo headed the car, fast, on the road out of town. Very fast. 'Gonna tell your grandmother?' asked David.

'Tell her what?'

'Where you're going. Where we're going.'

'Why?' Theo laughed.

'Well . . . nothing. I just thought . . .'

'You live your life your way, kid. I'll do the same with mine. Geddit?'

David relaxed. They didn't speak for several minutes. The hum of the motor of the near-new RX7, the competence of the driving and, above all, the close company of the driver were enough. They had travelled some distance when David said, 'That's where we shoot ducks,' and pointed.

Theo pulled the car, tyres screeching, to a half. 'Must see this. Where? Can't see no ducks.'

'Over that fence. Over the rise. Down in a dam. They'll be there.'

'Can we go'n see?'

'Sure.'

'Whose place is it? Yours?'

'Hell, no,' said David. 'Belongs to my uncle. Mum's brother. His daughter is Julie. The one in our class.'

'Yeah, yeah. Got it. The one who shivers when you stand by her.'

'Crap. Come on. Just walk up to the top of the hill. We won't go down. No sense in disturbing them,' said David.

'Sure gonna get disturbed real soon,' said Theo. 'Like big time disturbed.'

They sat on the hill-top under an old pine and looked down on the dam below. 'What you reckon?' asked David.

'Holy cow,' Theo shook his head. 'Look at 'em all. Thousands. Bet I could get a dozen with one blast.'

'How come?' David asked, and smiled to himself.

'They're so bloody close. Wouldn't stand a chance.'

'Oh. I see. You gonna shoot them on the water, eh?'

'Why not?'

'You're not allowed to,' said David.

Theo looked around. 'Who's to see? Except them,' he nodded down towards the ducks. 'And they won't be telling.'

'It's a sport, mate. Not outright murder,' said David.

Theo nodded again. 'What difference is it to the ducks? Poor suckers. They know it's a sport? Bloody stupid, if you ask me. You mean you gotta wait till they fly up in the air?'

'Yep.'

'Dumb,' said Theo. 'You couldn't hit 'em in the air.'

'Of course you can. Not easy. Guess that's why it's more er . . . fun. I don't wanna hit no ducks on the water. Mind you,' he laughed, 'seen Dad do it once or twice when he hasn't been getting any.'

'That's my sort of guy,' said Theo. 'How about you stay home and I'll go with him?' A flight of birds passed close over their heads. The beat of wings and the drawn-out, stretched 'Waaa-rk Waaa-rk' call of those on the water sounded into the air. 'Make the most of it, ducks,' said Theo. 'Not long now and I'll be eating you.'

'You should be so lucky,' said David. 'End up eating one in fifty of what you can see and you'd be doing okay. Even then a frozen chook from the supermarket tastes better! Come on. Let's go.'

The road narrowed as it climbed into the range of hills. The farms became rougher, the houses more widely separated. 'Where the hell does it go?' asked Theo.

'Nowhere,' said David. 'If you'd bothered to ask, or if you'd read the signposts, you'd know that. Pine forest up the end. Dad and me come up here hunting in summer.'

'Not for ducks?'

'No, smartarse. Not for ducks. Rabbits, hares. Heaps of goats,' said David.

'Jesus, you're a killer.'

'If you say so,' said David, and decided to rub it in. 'Got me a young deer up here. You know. Bambi? Seen the movie, eaten the meat.' Then he laughed. 'I'm only joking.'

'Reckon I'll have a go at calling you killer and not kid,' said Theo.

'Yeah. Slow down. This road soon stops even pretending to be one.'

'Yeah. You're right, killer.' Theo did not slow. The first dimness of dusk and falling shadow made the track difficult to see and harder to navigate. The car jolted and tossed across potholes and corrugations and slewed in and out of the ruts of rain run-off. Trees, scrub and scruffy pine, pressed in closer. 'Great!' Theo gunned, over-revved the engine. 'Wish I'd spotted this was here before now. You can keep your killing, killer. Me? I'm gonna be a rally driver.' He roared into a sharp, bridged curve and up a damp and shaded incline. Faster. 'Just pray nothing's coming the other way.'

The track broadened as he crested the hill and Theo accelerated the car into a wider curve. A sudden jolt.

An explosion; sharp, clear, loud. The car spun. Theo braked. Spun further, faster, out of control. 'For Christ sake!' yelled David. Once around, twice. Into a third spin. 'Jesus . . .'

Into a ditch. Into a bank. Full stop.

Neither boy spoke for a moment. They breathed deeply, gasping. Then came the relief. Theo started to laugh. A high-pitched, nervous, almost hysterical giggle. 'Shit!' he gasped. 'Shit shit shit,' he turned to David. 'You . . . you okay?'

'Sure,' said David, and then he, too, started to laugh.

The two of them laughed in one gigantic roaring of relief and defiance of danger. David braced himself against the dash and Theo, laughing more rationally now, reached out and covered David's hand with his. 'Sure you're all right, kid?' he asked.

The feel of the touch sobered both. They looked at each other, made no further move, looked away. David did not take his hand away and Theo edged his fingers into David's palm. They sat for a few moments, just holding hands. 'You're sure you're all right?' Theo repeated.

'Sure. Sure. You?' asked David. Slowly, very slowly he relaxed his hand, held for another few seconds and then withdrew it to himself.

'What am I doing in this place?' was all Theo said.

It was David who turned them both back to their immediate situation. 'Come on. We both gotta get out your side. This side's jammed up the bank. Better spot what damage. Gotta torch? It's getting dark.'

'Glovebox, I think. Pass my smokes. Can't say I don't need one now,' and he lit up. 'Whew! Bummer,' Theo laughed.

They got out. The car was wedged, but not too deeply,

into a ditch and against the bank at the side of the road. The rear off-side tyre was flat. Blow-out. 'God. We sure were lucky,' said David.

'Call this luck? What the hell we gonna do? Nearest farm must be an hour back on foot, more even. Take bloody hours to get a tow-truck up here.' Theo paced, nervous. 'God knows. Guess we better get walking.'

David stood back and looked at the car and then at the car's owner. He saw for the first time that Theo was not always the in-control and laid-back master of everything. 'Jesus, Theo,' he said. 'Not the end of the bloody world. No one has to walk anywhere. Sure you've winged it, but just a bit. You got a flattie and it's in a ditch. God, mate, we're not helpless and hopeless. Waddaya?' he giggled. 'A woossie? We'll push the bloody thing. No sweat. Take us twenty minutes, tops.'

He was right. The weight of the two was more than enough to manhandle the car onto the roadway. David changed the wheel. The whole thing took ten minutes. He stowed the jack and the flat-tyred wheel into the boot, slammed it shut and brushed off his hands on his shirt and jeans. 'Okay?' He looked at Theo.

'Yeah, kid . . . killer. I'm impressed. More to you than a pretty face,' said Theo. 'Guess we better get going.'

'Guess we better drive slow, too,' said David. 'Bet even your car doesn't come with two spare wheels.'

'You've made your point,' said Theo.

'God, if I had a car like this you wouldn't catch me flogging it up here the way you did,' said David.

'It's only a car,' said Theo.

'So . . . o, you've brought your friend? He can stay for dinner? You might have let me know, Theo,' said Gretel

Meyer.

'No, Gretel. I've brought him in to clean up before I drop him off back at his place. Got a flat tyre. Car's got a dent or two. Went into a bank.'

'Tsk, tsk. Boys! He can stay for dinner, no?'

'I had better get home, thank you,' said David.

'As you will,' said Gretel.

'No. You can stay for dinner,' said Theo.

'If he can't, he can't,' said Gretel.

'And if he can, he can,' said Theo. 'Phone home. Go on,' he said to David.

'Well . . .'

'Go on. D'you want me to do it?'

'Well, if it's all right.' David looked at Gretel.

'I've invited you, boy. Of course it is all right,' she said.

He phoned. It was all right. 'But don't be too late home, dear,' said his mother. 'What about your home-work?'

'None tonight, Mum,' he lied. 'Nothing I can't catch up on in the morning. Start with two study periods.'

'And don't forget to tell Mrs Meyer that any time she wants to come and see the garden, she's more than welcome. Not that there's much to see at the moment,' said his mother.

'Wanna shower?' asked Theo.

'Good wash'll do,' said David. 'For now.'

Theo looked at him with a slight smile. He said nothing.

'What are you grinning at me for?'

'Nothing. No reason at all. You're pretty handy with a car, kid,' said Theo.

'Oh, it's us hick-town guys, see. When we run out of stuff to shoot . . .'

'Yeah, yeah. Point taken. Anyway, thanks. Now I'm off to have a shower.' He smiled again at David. 'You stay and talk to Granny, if you like. You can talk about gardens and plants. Use the main bathroom when you feel like it. Towels and junk and everything in there.'

David enjoyed his five minutes in the bathroom and then joined Gretel Meyer.

'There's a glass of wine.' She nodded. 'Theo always has one. I'm sure you do, too.' She smiled at him.

'Sometimes,' he said.

'Sit down, boy. No no no,' she changed her mind, 'you have a look at my garden. You did not see much the last time you came.'

'But . . . it's dark,' said David.

'Aha,' she laughed. 'Look.' She pressed a switch and the long bank of velvet curtain glided back, exposing a wall of window and the terrace beyond. She pressed a further switch and the garden was flooded with light.

'Wow!' he breathed. 'Wonderful. It's . . . it's beautiful.'

'One day it will be,' said Gretel. 'Another five years, I think.' She smiled. 'When everything has grown to some size and to some shape.'

Three, four floodlight spots, well-sited and carefully directed, penetrated to light the whole. A series of low, mushroom-shaped standard lights surrounded the artificial lake. An artful pattern of full light, half light and shade played over the whole garden. David stood, speechless, at the marvel of it all.

'Come,' said Gretel. 'We'll go on the terrace. Bring your jacket. I think you do truly appreciate what it is I am trying to do.'

'I think I do,' said David, slowly. 'It is, I think, the loveliest garden I have seen. It's . . . it's . . .' He was lost

40

for words. 'Have you done all of this by yourself?'

'Yes, I have. Except for the earthmoving for the pond and the bank beyond.' She pointed.

'Well, you've done it real good. It's great.'

She pointed out features and talked about them and he followed as she walked the length of the terrace. 'The pond is simple. Water lilies. Iris of all sorts. Grasses, little flaxes among the rocks. The bank behind the pool — you see it? A little more cunning. A belt of birch, the ones with the papery white bark, and in the front a lot of liquidambar. Ah, even this year, so soon after planting, the colours of the autumn leaves are lovely. The bank towards the house. See?' She pointed again. 'The rhododendrons and camellias. Now, they are a little slow,' she laughed. 'Maybe just a little too slow for me. We shall see who wins. Time.' She spread her hands. 'The sheep dung may hurry them up. Now then, the bank on the other side. Just a hotch-potch of what I have always wanted to plant and, up there by my bedroom window, a clump of white lilac.' She stood still for a moment. 'A memory . . . a memory,' she repeated. 'As a child, outside the window of my room . . . Ah, how it scented the spring night air.'

'You just might lose a few of your rhodos,' said David.

'Why so?'

'Not the right soil for them round here. Not acid enough.'

'You do know your gardening,' said Gretel.

'Well, reckon you know all of that, anyway,' he said. 'Feed 'em acid stuff and a bit of the sheep sh . . . manure. Keep them mulched in summer. Still, guess you're doing that.'

'Yes, I am,' she laughed. 'Right down to the sheep shit.'

41

'Looks as if your lawn will need one more mow before we get into winter proper.'

'No,' said Gretel, smiling. 'And I do believe I've caught you out.' She pointed.

'How?' All of a sudden he felt less shy with the woman. 'How have you caught me out?' He followed her pointing.

'Not grass. Not lawn, boy. You are looking out on my thousands upon thousands upon back-breaking thousands of grape-hyacinths. Blue muscari. They come, already, all the baby leaves. You wait, David Mason. Just you wait until the spring comes. Then my lawn will be a carpet of deep, beautiful blue. Just you imagine, now, the night lights playing on that. My blue lawn.'

Theo was drinking. He drank with the same deliberation with which he drove, spoke, smoked. 'Had the guided tour, kid?' he looked up. 'Come on, old lady. Close the bloody windows and pull the curtains and stop showing off. I'm hungry.'

'Old lady, he calls me. Cheeky animal,' she chuckled. 'You can wait for your food. It's not ready. You pour me another drink. I want a sit-down.'

'If you didn't spend all your time admiring your blessed garden and watching each leaf grow, you wouldn't need to sit down and could get me my food on time,' said Theo.

'You'll be lucky indeed to get any food at all if you go on like this in front of our guest.' Gretel Meyer sat down. 'Theodore tells me you have resigned from your football?' She looked at David and raised an eyebrow.

'Yes,' he said.

'Seems a little pity seeing as you were excellent at it.'

David looked at Gretel and chose his words. 'Just because you are good at something doesn't always mean you want to go on doing it.'

'Hmm. Is that so? It would seem to me that those of us who are clearly not very good at very many things might see things differently. I think we find if we are lucky enough to be good at doing just one thing, well, we go on doing it.'

David did not know how to reply.

'So . . . o? What d'you say to this, my little prince?' Gretel's eye stayed on David. 'Eh?'

'Leave the kid alone, Granny,' said Theo, lighting a cigarette. 'Get off his case.'

'Someone of just about sixteen years who knows all about acid foods for rhododendrons is quite capable of dealing with what I might say, Theodore,' said Gretel.

'Shoot,' said Theodore. 'That, too? Manure and car engines? Whew!'

'Ah, Theodore,' said David, something telling him not to end up as either the net or the ball in this tennis match. 'Do I make you feel inadequate?'

They both looked at him. There was a second or two of silence and then they both laughed very loudly. 'Ha ha ha. More to this one, eh, than meets the eye. Hah!'

'As you say, Grandmama. Now, for God's sake let's have something to eat.' Theo did not take his eyes off David who, in return, stared straight back. The last of the laughter was on the faces of both of them, but it had not reached their eyes.

She might be a better gardener than anyone else he had ever come across, David thought, but Gretel Meyer was surely not one of the world's great chefs. David

43

was hungry and the odour of the cooking casserole tantalised.

Dinner was short and sharp. The casserole was overcooked, the meat both dry and hard. The potatoes were underdone and carrots, mixed with peas, had been boiled to a marbled and lumpy orange-green paste. Gretel ate swiftly, greedily, as if this meal were her last. Her eyes darted from plate to plate around the table. Finally she wiped her mouth, precisely and neatly, on a corner of her napkin and said, absently, 'Mmm. That was good.'

'Very nice, Mrs Meyer,' David said.

Theo looked at David and said nothing.

Gretel quickly loaded the dishwasher and made coffee which they took through with them to the livingroom. The whole exercise of dinner had taken less than fifteen minutes. Now they sat in silence, Gretel and her grandson seeming lost in private thoughts.

The whole thing, the whole set-up was alien to David. Dinner time at the Mason's was generally a long and noisy affair. This was the time when, coming together again, you shared what the day had given individually. A sharing that often continued for an hour or more after the meal had ended.

'So . . . o.' Again the dragged out word that seemed both comment and query. Gretel smiled vaguely at the two boys, but said no more.

David smiled politely and fossicked his mind for something to say. 'Where are you from, Mrs Meyer?' he asked.

'You must call me Gretel. I told you. I meant it.'

'Sorry,' he said, grimacing slightly. 'It's a bit hard for me to call someone of your . . . well, someone of . . .'

'Someone so very very old by her first name?' She

44

smiled at him. 'Of course, you are quite right. But I have asked that you do.'

'Anyway, it's not Mrs Meyer. It's Miss Meyer, if you wanna get it right,' said Theo, quietly, not looking at either of them.

'Oh. I'm sorry. I thought . . .' David was confused.

'No matter, child. Be quiet Theodore,' said Gretel.

'Well, he should get it right. Shouldn't he Grandmama?'

'I'll Grandmama you,' she said.

'It's Mrs van Gelden. Or something like that,' said Theo.

'Stop now, Theo.' She spoke sharply. 'Pour us more coffee.'

At least the coffee was good. Very good. 'Yes, please, Theo,' David said, an innocent smile in the direction of the other.

'I'm from Auckland, my dear,' said Gretel.

'Hah!' said Theo. 'As if that's what he . . .'

'Don't listen to my rude and insolent and very lazy grandson, David.'

David sensed he was being directed along a certain path. 'It's just your voice, your accent. I thought you might be from, well, overseas?'

The woman sighed. 'Of course. I see. I was born in Poland. It is forty, more, years ago I came here with my baby, Theo's mother.'

'Why did you choose to come here?'

'My dear,' she smiled. 'Choice? Ah, you are so young. It was good I found anywhere to take us in. Shall we just say it was a time of turmoil.'

'Have you ever been back to see Poland again?' asked David.

She sat very quietly, her fingers plucking at the fabric of the chair arm. She looked at David and smiled

45

slightly. 'No,' she said. 'No. I have not been, as you say, to see Poland again.'

'Just thought you might have,' said David. Couldn't be money, he thought to himself. So, why not? After all, most of the friends of his parents, English, Scots or Irish born, seemed to travel back at least occasionally to catch up with family, see old places. 'Have you any family in Poland?' he asked. 'You know, to sort of go and see?'

Theo sat, all the while, half-closed eyes, half smile. Gretel Meyer drank her coffee. 'No,' she said, with an air of finality. 'No. I have no family to go to see. Now, you, young man, you tell me about you. Well, maybe just a little more than I know already.'

'No use, Granny.' Theo stirred himself. 'You know it all already. Like he was born in the cottage hospital 15.999 years ago and his old man runs that shop and his old lady . . .'

'You!' said his grandmother.

David looked at her. 'You could go back and see the lilac bush. Couldn't you?'

'What?' She looked at him blankly.

'The white lilac. The one that grew outside your bed-room window and scented the spring night air.'

She continued to look at him. She was very still. Finally, smiling, she said, 'Yes, Yes, I could,' and she stood. 'Excuse me, my dears. I think I shall have an early night. Theo, please be sure to look after David.'

He drove the car fast back into town. Almost on the outskirts he slammed on the brakes. Very hard. They skidded into a rest area. Stopped dead.

'You don't learn, do you?' said David.

Theo lit a cigarette. 'Sure you don't want one?'

'Christ, I'm having one anyway, every time you do and whether I want to or not.' David coughed and opened the window.

'Sorry,' said Theo.

'You will be. One day,' said David. 'Why have we stopped?'

They had sat on, mostly in silence, after Gretel Meyer had gone to her room. They had drunk a can of beer each before Theo had offered to drive him home. It was not late.

'Have you ever been with a girl?' Theo stared straight ahead through the windscreen and into the night.

'I had a girlfriend, yeah. Was last year. She left town in the long holidays,' said David. 'Not long before you turned up here. No one since.'

'That's not what I mean. You know what I mean. Don't you?' A snarl. 'Shit! You must know what I mean.'

'I know what you mean,' said David. 'No. I haven't been with a girl.'

'Bloody virgin. Most guys I know have had at least one go by your age.'

'I haven't. Have you?'

Theo turned to him. 'Yes, if you must know. More'n one. Yep.'

'So?'

'Yeah. So what?' Theo turned back to stare straight ahead again. Then, slowly, he rested his head on his hands on the steering wheel. His body started to tremble then wracked itself, shaking into hoarse, harsh sobs.

'Hey.' David reached out a hand and touched Theo's arm.

Theo reacted, shot, 'Don't touch me! Don't you touch me.'

'What?'

Theo calmed. 'Are you really so bloody thick? Are you? Don't you know what's happening?' He raised his head and looked at David. 'Little goodie duck-slaying football boots! God Almighty! I bet you even go to church on Sundays. Why the hell did I come here? You! You!!' And he was furious with a cold, hard anger. 'With your great big wide, innocent eyes. Mr Nice-Guy-don't-tread-on-the-bloody-daisies or on the feelings of anyone or anything unless it's a duck or a pig or a deer or a bloody stuffing alligator or whatever else crap crawls round here.' He laughed with no humour.

'Shut up!' yelled David. 'You shut up or I'll hit you hard. Harder'n I did last time, mate. I'm not bloody thick. I'm not. And I do know what's going on and I don't know why and I don't know what to do about it, either, and that's the fuckin' truth.'

'You do know?' Suddenly a quiet surprise. 'You? You know what's going on?'

'Yes. Of course I do. It seems to me it's you doesn't understand,' said David.

'God! I dunno. You bumble along, just as I expect you to and then, whammo, you up and surprise me. You've done it before.'

'Look, Theo. I dunno how to say any of this. I don't understand. No.' He put out a hand. 'Don't get me wrong. I know what it is. I know all the words. Jesus! I've been round changing rooms for bloody ever. I sure have heard all the words. God, I was always with older guys. Look, mate, I've used all the words. Was using them before I even knew what most of them meant. You should . . . Nah. Doesn't matter.'

'Go on,' said Theo, urgently.

'Can't say it all, can I? I'd puke on the words. All I do

48

know is that most of the guys I know, all of them probably, well . . . they'd have our nuts off if they knew.'
Pause. 'Or worse.'

'Gee whizz, kid.'

'Don't get smart, Theo. This is real hard for me, too.
Look, I've thought about it all. Do you know, I've even
looked real right up close all over my body. I'm all there.
I know it's all there and I know it's all in the right places
and I do not look any different from any other guy.'

'You look better'n most, kid.'

David ignored him. 'See, the answer's not there and
I don't know, I dunno where it is.'

'You don't mind?'

'God help us! Mind? Who's the thick one? Mind? It's
bloody killing me. I'm sick with it. Geddit?' He paused
and rubbed with a finger against the misting window
of the car. 'I ache. Do you know that? Bursting, sort of,
all the time.' He looked at Theo in a quick nervous glance
and continued, 'Don't you bloody dare say anything
smart.' Another pause. 'And you thought I didn't know?
Simple, you reckon I am. What you call me? Hick town
hunk? I've known since first I saw you. You know what?'

'What? Go on. Surprise me a bit more.' Theo lit another cigarette.

'Jesus! I hate you smoking. I knew about you, too.'

'How come? Bloody rot.'

'That night in the changing room. Why did you wait,
eh? Go on. Why? Then, after I smashed your face in,
why did you ring me up? Come on, Theo. Wasn't all
your fault. We both hung round and we both knew why.'

Theo pointed. 'There's a hip-flask of whisky in the
glovebox. Get it out. You want a slug?'

'Sure do,' said David. 'You shouldn't carry booze in
a car. It's asking for trouble.' He hunted around, found

the flask, unscrewed the cap, took a long gulp, coughed, choked, swigged again and handed it on to Theo. 'There.'

'God. You're gonna have to get past your parents somehow. You'll sure stink of smoke as well as the piss,' said Theo.

'Least of my problems,' said David. 'But I better be getting home. Like, I know it's a helluva laugh to you but I don't get off on Mum and Dad worrying. I don't.'

'I know you don't and I'm not laughing. Like, well, tonight with the car. I think I'd have liked it better when I told old Gretel about the car if she had . . . doesn't matter. God knows, though, they'd all have a heap to worry about if they knew, all of them.'

'I thought you were a right shit,' said David.

'I am, kid.'

'Nah. No you're not. See, I haven't been worrying about you. Not one bit. I think you just taught me a lesson,' said David.

'Come off it, kid.'

'Come off it, kid, crap! All what you've said, now, in the car, tells me something. Sure, you've been worrying about yourself. But you been worrying about me, too. I'm right?'

'So? Where to from here?'

David looked sideways at Theo. 'Oh, I dunno. Reckon it's about time you lit yourself another smoke,' he laughed. 'I'm learning, see. That's the sort of thing you'd say.'

'Quick learner.'

'I know two things,' said David.

'Yeah?'

'If I touched you right now, well, first off, I wouldn't know much what to do and, second, I wouldn't know how to stop doing what it is I didn't know what to do if

I did get started.'

'It might be,' said Theo, very slowly, 'that there isn't anything to be done between us. Not now. Not ever. Who knows? It does seem to me, but, that the least we can do is go on seeing each other. I think that's some sort of help.'

'You, too, eh?'

'Me too what?'

'It doesn't seem quite so bad when we're together. When we get to see each other and be together.'

'You're right, David.'

5

There was no way that Jack Mason was going to allow his son to introduce a complete stranger into the established ritual of duck shooting's opening morning. David did not even waste time asking. In the event it didn't matter. Gretel Meyer ordered Theo to Auckland to have his car repaired.

'Nothing much I can do about it. It belongs to her, anyway. She's got a tame panelbeater up there. Take my word for it, her car needs it more than mine. Granny isn't the world's greatest driver,' Theo had said.

'Wondered why she didn't give you heaps for what you done to it.'

'I'll be back about Tuesday. You can give me a duck shoot shopping list. Gotta have the gear.'

'You gotta gun licence?' David had asked.

'Thought you got me there, eh?' Theo said. 'Yeah. I have. Last school I went to. Picked shooting as a sport for the excellent reason that no bloody exercise was involved. Was all part of that. Never thought I'd need the bloody thing. Now, tell me what I gotta get.'

'It'll cost you an arm and a leg, Theodore.'

'My family might be short of people but we're not short of money,' Theo said.

'Where d'you get it all? The money?'

'Hot-water bottles. Mind your own business. Can I get you anything?'

'Yep. I want a new Beretta top of the line shotgun. Maybe a Browning. Dunno. Bring two or three back so I can try them out and don't forget I've got long arms.' David grinned. 'Don't go above say, three, four thousand. Okay?'

'Piss off,' Theo had said.

The ritual had been set in place for years. David shot with his father and his uncle on his uncle's farm. Father and son would arrive the night before, check gear, clothing, guns. Talk about seasons gone and prospects for the coming morning. Helped by his aunt, they would prepare and pack food and take off, very early, to bed and spend a restless night counting minutes, hours, until four-thirty or five the next morning.

This morning was the answer to a duck shooter's prayer. Misty and with a drizzle of light rain, cold and with little wind and not a ray of light in the morning sky when, at five-thirty, they set off across the paddocks. Three men and Digger, the dog. No talk apart from the occasional, muffled grunt. And so to their mai-mai, their hide, their duck-blind, staggering along overloaded with guns, ammunition and a full pack of food and drink. Into the sounds of their quarry as the birds, sensing the approach of morning, awoke, called, quarrelled, beat wings.

Into the hideaway with a good twenty, thirty minutes before the start of shooting and a settling into the cold, damp security and camouflage of the blind. Then waiting, cold, shivering and ready, all ears on the growing noise out on the pond. Checking watches for the appointed time. Then the first distant shots from other guns echoed in now from the ponds and dams and streams of the surrounding district. 'Let's go. Let's shoot,' whispered the uncle as, in the grey light, he spotted the sight of a flock of twelve, twenty or more birds, circling high and then low and then coming into land on the water.

They shot. A first volley, almost in unison from the three guns.

David shot with a sure and certain ease, confident. The gundog, Digger, swam and retrieved, as excited in his work as were the shooters. A quick, casual and brutal breaking of the necks of the wounded. Elation. 'It'll be a bloody good morning,' said his uncle. 'Fat buggers, too.'

The pond emptied of ducks. More flew in. Emptied. Filled. Shoot. Wait. Shoot. Wait. Time for food.

'Shooting better this year. Know I am,' said Jack Mason. 'Spot on.'

David said nothing. He sat back, ate and waited and eyed, examined a clutch of their victims as they lay limp, dead, a faint breeze fluttering into false life the feathers of a couple. Blood.

On into the morning and a lethal repetition and a growing mound of dead birds. 'Great shooting, Jack. God, that bugger was out of range. Good one!'

David was the killer. He had known this for the past couple of seasons. It was never acknowledged by the older two. With a sure accuracy and fine timing he would bring the birds down and his father and uncle would score them as their own. At first it had puzzled him, but then he understood. He said nothing. 'The older I get, the better I seem to shoot,' his father had said to his mother. 'Would never have believed it.'

It didn't worry David. Indeed he had come to think

of the synchronising of his actions with those of the older pair as being part of the whole business. When it didn't quite come off it didn't matter. Those times simply provided him with a tally of his own.

They shot for most of the morning. Grey, mallard, paradise, a satisfactory haul. They drank coffee, well laced with bourbon, and ate bacon and egg pie, well laced with rain. They sneezed and coughed in the chill and did not stop their killing game until the flights of well-confused and wary birds thinned and the shooting became more difficult in the clear grey light of late morning. They stretched their legs.

'Call it a day?'

'Best bloody opening I can remember.'

'Must be six, seven years since . . .'

'Good shooting, Davy,' said his uncle. 'Turning into quite a shot. 'Nother season or two be as good as your old man.'

Satisfied, they heaved home their haul.

It took much longer for the three of them to pluck, gut and pack their quarry for the freezer than it had for them to bring it down from the skies. A messy business. The more the shooting, the more the mess.

'My sympathy is, and always has been, on the side of the ducks. If you guys want to eat stringy flesh and mouthfuls of lead you're more than welcome.' David's aunt turned down their generous invitation to lend them a hand.

A memorable day.

The following Tuesday and David biked to the Meyer house. Theo had not returned. Gretel Meyer was in her garden. 'He will be back tonight. It took longer to get the right panel for his car than I was told. He will drive down tonight. I think it is tomorrow you and he have some sort of test at school. Right?'

'Right. It's a maths one.'

'So . . .o? What have you been up to, young man?'

'Shooting. Ducks,' he said.

'Ah. Of course. I hear the banging away all round here. Silly. Well, then. Where is the duck you have brought me? Eh?' she laughed. 'Is that not the custom?'

'I thought you might like to wait until next week. Next week and Theo can bring you plenty.'

'That one? Hah! I should be so lucky. He tells me you will take him with you,' said Gretel.

'Yep. It's holidays, then. Be plenty of time for it. It'll be cool.'

'I shall be chasing him to study rather than him chasing those ducks. He needs his exams this year. Mind you, should I succeed it will be the first time ever.'

'I promise, Mrs Meyer . . . er . . . Gretel. I'll make him do some work.'

'You!' she laughed. 'Forgive me for saying, boy, but better people than you have tried and failed.'

'I'll give it my best shot,' said David.

'It's his best shot that concerns me. Save yours for those stupid ducks. Now, then. If you have nothing better to do you can help me with these rocks and then we'll have coffee. Right?'

'Sure,' he said. 'I said you should sing out if you ever need a hand. I'd like to help. These rocks are much too heavy for you to lump around.'

She laughed again at him. 'I may be old, boy, but one foot in the grave I have not got. The exercise is good and I have done far, far harder work in my time

56

than this little lot of rocks.'

Gretel Meyer was building a rockery at one corner of her pond with a curve of wall to one side. She was building the wall from broken slabs of old concrete, piled one upon the other. 'Much more where I get this. It is from your rubbish dump. A man there told me it was from old footpaths of the town. I can manage three, four pieces at a time in my car.'

'You put that stuff in your car?' David sounded horrified.

'A car is to use, boy.'

'My Mum's on the council,' he said. 'I'll get her to see if one of the trucks can bring it straight out to you here.'

'I should have thought of that for myself,' said Gretel.

'No sweat,' said David.

'Just you use some sweat now and get this lot down there. Then we'll see about this truck or whatever.'

Gretel made the most of her labourer. He heaved concrete and rolled boulders for an hour. For a further hour he shovelled dirt, at her direction, into the nooks and crannies of her rockery. He rested on his spade. 'What you gonna plant in it?'

'Narcissus,' she said. 'I found in Auckland a lovely, lovely selection of miniature rockgarden bulbs. Beautiful. Your father should stock them.'

'Yeah. You'd be the only person in town who'd buy them. Well, you and Mum and she's not the best paying customer we've got.'

'Stop resting on your spade. There is a bank of hydrangea I want planted in and around the rhododendrons. You do a little bit of digging, eh?'

He dug.

'You stay for dinner? Theo will be back shortly.'

'No. No thanks,' quickly. He could smell another casserole. 'Thanks a lot er . . . Gretel. It's this test tomorrow. I've sure got to work at it.'

'Coffee, then. You have done enough hard labour.'
They walked up to the house. 'See. Its leaves have now
all gone.'

'From what?' He was puzzled.

'The white lilac. Sit there.' She pointed at a stone
bench. 'I'll bring the coffee out. It's a good evening.'

When she came back with the coffee he asked her,
'Your garden here, well . . . the white lilac and the blue
lawn . . .'

'Yes?'

'Are you trying to copy what you had at your home
when you were little? You know, back when you were
in Poland?'

'No no no, boy. Of course not. Just the white lilac. It
is — how should I put it? — a remembrance.'

'Rosemary is for remembrance. Mum says that,' said
David.

'I think many people have, David. Many people have
said it. You love plants? Yes, I know you do.'

'I've already told you that, Gretel,' said David.

She looked out into her garden and smiled. 'Yes. So
you have,' and they sat together drinking their coffee.
'There was only the white lilac. There was no garden.
We lived in a village. Well, I think you would call it a
town. Old houses. Tall. Narrow streets and many people,' she laughed. 'Not enough room, there was, for all
the people, much less gardens. A town from a picture
book of fairy tales for children. Hah! Some fairy tale.'
She paused for a moment. 'Cobblestone and crooked
old houses. We had just the lilac tree and once a year it
was like a glorious gift.' She turned away from him.

'The perfume. The scent in the air . . . comes to me now over so long a time. But the picture I see is not the lilac. No. I see the faces . . . I see the faces . . .'

'Who . . . who do you see?'

Gretel Meyer picked up the coffee pot and refilled their cups. 'I see my sisters. Hannah. Sarah. My father. My aunt. My aunt Esther. I had no mother. My mother died when Sarah was born. My great-aunt Esther. She was the aunt of my father.'

'And they've all gone? They've all died?' David asked.

'Yes, my dear. They've all gone.'

'What did your father do?'

'Do? Oh, I see. For a living? He was a grain merchant. So was his father before. Buy grain, sell grain. Wheat. Millet. Barley. Whatever. We lived above the store. It was no big business, I think. Hah! I am no longer sure.'

'Did you . . .?' he began.

'Enough,' she interrupted, softly. 'It is getting dark now and you must cycle. You should go. First, let me pay you.'

David's face worked, puzzled. 'Pay me for what?'

'For all your hard work. I could not have done as much without your young back, shoulders and arms.'

'No way. You're not paying me Mrs er . . . Gretel. You pay me and I won't help you again. That's a promise.'

He turned at the gate and looked back at the tiny figure on the terrace. He waved. Her eyes were on him, he knew. She did not wave in return.

6

Shooting with Theo made David thankful he had not asked his father if this friend could join in with them on opening morning.

'This is a very boring sport,' said Theo, and got up for a walk around. Six ducks overhead, getting ready to land, were quickly and clearly alerted. They flew off.

'This is a very uncomfortable sport.' Another walk around. 'This is a ridiculous sport. I thought we were meant to catch ducks, not bloody pneumonia. D'you think your uncle would mind if I shot that sheep?'

'Sheep don't fly,' said David, wearily.

'I'll make it,' said Theo.

A sole bird which, David thought, could only have been stone-deaf and simple-minded, flew in. 'It's yours,' he whispered. 'Shoot.'

Theo let forth with a war-cry of exuberance. He half stood, fumbled with his gun and shot right across David, harmlessly into the water. The bird was safe and David enraged. 'Christ! You coulda killed me. As it is you've bloody done for my eardrums!' He was shaking.

Theo pulled a face. 'Gee, kid. I did what you said.' He looked and sounded concerned.

'It's okay. Look. Listen to me,' and David went

through the lecture again, wondering that anyone, anyone at all, much less this know-it-all at his side, could be so thick. He eyed, envious, Theo's gear. What a waste! 'Look. Give us those three empty drink cans. I'll throw 'em up. You stand. Follow through my throw like I've shown you. Then give it a blast when you think the can's up to its highest.'

'Yeah. And no ducks'll come in, then. You said we gotta be quiet,' said Theo.

'Look, mate. Any ducks thinking of coming you're not going to get, anyway,' said David. 'Have a bit of practice and then we'll stalk up to another little dam further up. Should get you something there.'

Six sticks, three cans, five clods of earth and Theo fluked one hit. 'Stupid sport,' and Theo lit a cigarette.

'Shooting with you might be the one thing that'd make me take up smoking,' said David. 'You reckon it calms the nerves and I reckon mine are shattered.'

They climbed to the second dam, coming down onto it through scrubby growth and fern. They rested for a minute and David parted the growth to look down on the water. There were no birds on the pond but two paradise duck ambled, grazed up on the further bank. He mimed to Theo who whispered, 'You have a go. I'll just watch.'

The curious cry of the birds, as much goose as duck, told David they had become aware of danger. He stood, ready to fire as they lifted into the air, hovering a little and then planing to escape. One shot. A hit. Second shot. No great chance. A lucky hit. Both birds fell, one in a stone-dead plummet, the other winged. David cornered and killed the second bird, retrieved the first. 'You have them.' He passed the birds to Theo. 'Glad I got them both,' he said, simply. 'Don't suppose you know but they live in pairs, mate for life.'

Theo gulped, said nothing. He kept his eye on David.

They waited on in the clear, rising morning, but nothing landed and they walked, loud and laughing back to the main pond and towards the road. 'SSshh . . .' David restrained Theo. 'Take it slow. Quiet. Could surprise one or two back here.'

A small flock paddled. Four or five birds. Theo bagged his duck. He thrust his gun at David and went to get it where it floundered, still alive, in reeds at the pond's edge. It tried to escape his clutch but he was too quick and he lifted it, flapping. 'What do I do? What do I do now?'

'Kill it,' called David. 'Don't let it . . .'

'Can't . . . don't know . . .'

'Break its neck. Hurry up,' said David.

'You do it.'

'No way.' Flat. 'You wound it, you kill it.' He raised his voice. 'Get a move on.'

Theo killed the duck, dropped it and wiped bloodied hands on his trousers. He swallowed hard, once, twice, looked away. Walked to the water and washed his hands.

'You've never, ever killed anything before, have you?' David spoke softly.

'So what?' Rough.

'So nothing. It's okay,' said David.

'Look at it.' Theo nudged the dead bird with the toe of his boot. 'The . . . the thing's so bloody beautiful.'

'Yeah.'

'I'll do it again,' he said slowly. 'I'll do it again. It's sort of exciting. Look at all the colours on its feathers. Just look.'

'Yeah. Beautiful,' said David. 'Come on, red-neck,

hick-town killer. We'll go home. Bring your duck. Its lovely feathers and all its guts'll make great fertiliser under one of Gretel's shrubs. Then I'll show you how to cook it.'

'I'm not gonna eat it,' said Theo. 'Hey. You're not gonna make me get its guts out?'

'Can't wait to see that bit,' said David.

'I'm not gonna eat it,' Theo repeated.

'Then stuff the bloody thing, mount it and shove it on your bedroom wall,' said David.

'God, you're hard,' said Theo.

'Sure am,' said David. 'Ducks eat frogs. We eat ducks. I think frogs are a choice colour of green. Wonder what a duck thinks as he eats one. Come on. It's cold.'

David turned sixteen. 'If you want a party you can have one,' said his mother.

'I don't think I do,' said David.

Maureen Mason looked at her son. 'I'm surprised. Why not? You've always had one in the past.'

'Maybe next year,' he said. 'It's not all that easy any more. If I invite the rugby guys, and I know they'd come . . . well, see, they're all older. Seventeen, eighteen, some of them. They'd expect booze. You know that.'

'Yes. I know what you mean,' she said.

'And don't get me wrong, Mum. I'd like it, too. Reckon I've got about a snowball's chance of being allowed, eh?'

'You're right,' she said, very firmly. 'We're not about to break open the liquor cabinet for you. Not just yet. Not this year.'

'Nor next year, either,' he muttered.

'What about your own age plus a few of the younger

ones?' she asked.

'Geez, Mum! That's what the rugby did. You know that. Yeah, so I know the younger ones, but I'm not about to invite them to a party.' He glanced at his mother and smiled. 'Besides, they'd want booze, too.'

'I don't believe it.' Maureen Mason shook her head. 'It's only yesterday I taught most of them.'

'We grew up, Mother.'

'Hmm. Far too fast. I can't win.'

'You know what I'd really like?'

'Tell me.' She threw up her hands 'An orgy?'

'What's that?'

'It doesn't matter. Come on. Tell me what you'd like?'

'Just dinner with you and Dad and Janet, too, if she can come down on her days off. Better have the rellies. Aunty Janet and Uncle Dick and Julie. And I'd like to invite Theo and his grandma.'

'Quite a cocktail,' said Maureen Mason. 'What's that? About nine or ten? I guess I can do it if you give me a hand. Wouldn't do it for anyone else, mind.' She smiled at him. 'Might even be able to ask old Mrs Meyer a bit earlier and she and me can toddle around the garden you tell me she's so keen on seeing.' She looked at her son as they sat together at the kitchen table. 'You're suddenly very friendly with this boy, Theo,' she said quietly.

'Yeah. So what? I like him.' He knew he sounded defensive and was sensing a criticism that was, quite likely, not even in her words.

'He's . . . well, very mature for his years. Very personable.'

'Dunno,' David shrugged. 'What's personable?'

'Never mind, dear. I'm sure you know what you're doing. And he's certainly very pleasant the times he's

64

been round here. It's just . . . well, to be honest, he doesn't seem quite your type.' She raised her eyebrows. 'I know he smokes.'

'A lot of the guys do, Mum.' It was David's turn to sigh. 'Bloody idiots. Even I did, once.'

'Yes, my love. When you were seven years old and you were violently ill. And the way he drives that little car . . . Oh, well, I'm sure he's very nice, dear.' She stood and ruffled his hair. 'Any friend of yours just must be,' she laughed.

'Wouldn't bet on it, Mum,' he said.

He walked out to the Meyer house to give his invitation. It had been a couple of days since he had seen Theo and the silence puzzled him. Once he had phoned. There had been no reply.

The house looked shut up. The day was cold, very cold, so this in itself did not surprise him. The doors of the garage were closed and there was no sound of radio, stereo, or television. David reached the conclusion that both Gretel and Theo were away. He turned to leave, but decided to have a look around the garden. He pulled up the hood of his jacket, stuck his hands into the pockets and began a slow wander around the property, stooping now and again to examine labels on shrubs and trees. He pressed with his toe the earth around those that were newly planted and cleared excesses of dead leaf from the smallest of the bulbs that were now breaking through the cold earth.

David examined the white lilac outside the window of Gretel's bedroom. The very last of summer leaves clung, dead, to its branches while the slightest of thickening at stem ends hinted at approaching spring. He looked long and hard at the lawn. No trace of blue as yet.

He dawdled his way around the garden, the place that had already cast some spell on him. In his mind's eye he could see what, one day, the whole would be. David sat for a couple of minutes on the stone bench and smiled at a lone duck ferretting the edges of Gretel's pond. 'Don't let Theo see you, mate. Not even he could miss you from his bedroom.' He clapped his hands. 'Go on. Get out! Bet the sod would shoot you on the water.' The duck cocked its head, seemed to eye him, paddled out a little but did not fly. 'What the hell tells you you're safer here? Eh? Must be something.' He stood and did another circuit of the house before walking off down the drive. Theo's voice stopped him.

'You call on people you're supposed to knock. Aren't you going to knock?'

'I did.' And you must have heard, mate, thought David.

'Was out the back. Come in, if you want.'

'Where's Gretel?'

'Auckland. Meeting. She's back tomorrow.'

'When did she go?'

'Weekend.'

'You didn't phone.'

'Been a bit crook.'

'What's wrong?' And you're a liar, too, mate.

'Dunno. Something I ate, I guess. Pneumonia from the duck shooting.' Theo managed a smile. 'For God's sake come in. Freeze my balls off out here.' He shivered.

The sitting room was like an oven. Sliding doors closed and curtains pulled. The place was a mess. Half a dozen ashtrays overflowed on furniture and carpet and the packaging of every takeaway food outlet in the town littered the floor. A brandy bottle, near empty, and three or four glasses had left a pattern of rings on the whole length of a long, low table. The place stank.

'Shit!' said David. 'You sure it's been just two days?'

'Stick it, kid.'

'Want a hand to clean up?'

'When I want you to bloody housekeep for me I'll fish you out an apron.'

'I . . . I'm . . .'

'Never asked you to come out here.'

'You asked me in,' said David, quietly.

'Get out! Go on! Piss off!' Theo stood, face contorted, swollen, enraged. 'Get out! And take this, you little bastard, remember me by.' He aimed a foot and struck a vicious kick in the direction of David's groin. His anger, his upset made the effort futile and he kicked into thin air. With only the slightest effort David simply took Theo's leg and tripped him to the floor, stood back and looked down.

'Jesus!' Theo lunged from his knees, flung both arms around David's legs and the two of them were on the floor in a desperate gouging, heaving tussle that cleared the table of the brandy, the glasses, all of the ashtrays and upended several chairs. They gasped, tearing at each other in a flaring, spitting rage. They coursed the room one way and then the other in a fever of rolling, pounding motion. Free arms punched, free feet kicked, free fingers bit into flesh.

As fast as it had started it finished. One moment fury and in the next fully spent. They lay, still holding each other and fighting for breath. Their eyes held, continued to hold and then each, bodily, sank into the grasp of the other. Finally they relaxed and lay on their backs holding hands.

Eventually they turned towards each other and, at the same time, smiled. Theo lifted a hand and brushed lightly at David's forehead. 'Should see yourself. Just should look at yourself.'

'Should smell your breath,' said David. 'You okay?'

'Now? Yep. Yes I am. You?'

'I grew up in a rugby scrum. Remember?'

'Yeah. So you did.'

'Reckon you better fish out two of them aprons, eh?' David surveyed the room.

They laughed. As they had rolled the room in rage they now did the same in laughter and the mess grew greater. Then, together, they set the place to rights and worked, apronless, in a fever of energy.

'The old girl'll never know,' said Theo, admiring their efforts.

'Your old girl isn't that thick,' said David. 'Bet she spots something. She's bound to count her glasses and check her booze.'

'Gretel doesn't work that way. Can you stay?'

'Yes. I'll ring Mum and say I'm out here for dinner.'

'Hey, can I cook my duck?'

'Piss off. We've eaten so many at home I've got lead fillings up as far as my ears.'

'Let's have a shower. We both could do with one. Come on.' Theo looked at David.

'Okay.'

They ate one of Gretel's casseroles, microwaved into a sort of half life. 'Your grandma sure does some strange cooking,' said David.

'Does she?' Theo sounded surprised. 'I dunno. Maybe she does. Never really take much notice. I do know she's not really interested in food or in cooking. Mum says

Gretel eats to stay alive. That's it. Sometimes, if she's got a good book or she's having a great time out in the garden she never eats at all unless I remind her. Often she forgets to feed me. That's okay. Just get it for myself. King of the burgers, is me.'

Early evening. Both boys wore long towelling robes. David's clothes had been through the washing machine and were now tumbling dry. They sat, side by side, on the floor of the sittingroom. 'Wanna drink?' asked Theo.

'Thanks. Cup of tea.'

'I didn't mean that,' said Theo.

'I did,' said David. 'Can't keep up with you on the other.'

'Practice. That's all you need.'

'Yeah? Practice I can do without,' said David.

Theo made tea for them both. 'You win. I'll give up the booze,' he laughed. 'For you.'

'And smoking?'

'Have a heart.'

'Guess I can't win 'em all,' said David.

'Shut up and listen,' ordered Theo. 'You know when I went up to Auckland? For the car and the shooting stuff?'

'Yes.'

'I stayed over an extra day,' said Theo.

'I know that. Gretel told me it took an extra day to get the new door or the trim, whatever.'

'Wasn't that,' said Theo. 'When Gretel orders a new bit for a car, like, well, she gets it the day before yesterday. No. I went and saw this guy I know. Old guy. Mum's age. Friend of hers I've known him for years.'

'So?'

'He's a psychologist. Prisons, mainly. Anyway, Mum's known him for ages. Once they were real close. Was soon after my father died.'

'I didn't know your father was dead,' said David.

'Well he is, but this isn't about him. Happened years ago. I think I was six. Car crash. He was pissed. Look.' Theo shook his head. 'None of this is about him. I went and saw this guy, see. Felt I needed to talk to someone about you and me and mostly about my feelings.'

'You . . . you told him about us?'

'Didn't say any names. Don't worry,' said Theo.

'Well, you didn't have to, did you? He knows half of them already. Why couldn't you just talk to me?'

Theo looked at David. 'I couldn't. It had to be someone, someone else,' he said.

'Look, mate. This happened a little while back. How come you never told me?'

'Do you want to hear what he said or just argue about me saying it to him? Eh?'

'Yeah. I do want to hear,' said David.

'Then I'll say it again,' said Theo. 'Shut up and listen.'

Theo spoke quietly. For the most part he looked straight ahead, glancing now and then to see if David was listening. 'He told me that the feelings you'n'me have are very common. Reckons research shows that over half of all guys have these sorts of feelings, mainly just when they're younger, for another guy. It's the same with girls, you know, with girls. Nothing wrong about it. He says a helluva lot never sort of admit to it being anything more than a close friendship. At the end of it all some stay that way, attracted only to their own sex. He says it seems to be about one in ten.' He paused for a moment. 'Seems as if nothing is as simple and clearcut as all that, though. With some it is just a phase that's worked through or worked out. With others, as I say, it's gay the whole way. And there are a heap of others who can go both ways. Then, no matter which you pre-fer, there are even more ways of expressing what that relationship is. Then he went into all the stuff about it doesn't matter what you do providing it is right for you and right for who you are with and that you don't harm each other. God knows how you work that out. I dunno. Oh yeah. Then he got into what the law says. You know, all the crap about being sixteen.'

Theo stopped speaking. He reached for his cigarettes and lit one and drank from his cold cup of tea. He seemed to be waiting for David to speak, but David said nothing. 'He did say nothing was simple as all that and both you'n'me know that. He said to many people and a helluva lot in some strict churches, it's not right. It's dead wrong and a load of filth and against things in the Bible.' He paused before asking, 'You go to church?'

'Sometimes. Never heard anything about it in our church,' said David. 'I sang in the choir when I was just a little kid. Got dressed up in a cassock and a white surplice. One of my grannies said I looked like an angel.'

Theo grunted. 'Shoulda guessed. Kick 'em in the guts on Saturday, or plug 'em with lead. Sing a load of hymns on Sunday. Yep.'

'It's not like that,' said David. 'Anyway, my voice broke.'

'I've seen the evidence of that,' said Theo, grinning.

'I got big very quickly.'

Theo smiled more widely. 'It happens.' Then he got serious again. 'See, it's more than just that and it scares me a bit. Scares me shitless.'

'What does?'

'See, I don't want to live with the idea that I'm a

queer and that I'll always feel like this. Maybe you're the only guy I'll ever come across who . . . and, let's face it, we won't last forever. Things don't work that way. We're too different.'

'I see,' said David. 'You're sort of telling me it's over before we really get into it, before we done anything. You're telling me it's you setting all the rules.'

'Okay. So there's a one in a million chance we'll still be close in twenty years' time. That's not really what I meant,' said Theo.

'Mum and Dad have always said that we are what we are and it's the job of each of us to make the best of it,' said David.

'Holy shit! I don't think Mum and Dad were talking about what we're talking about,' said Theo. 'And you're getting me off the track. What I said was I don't think I can live easy with the thought of always being this way.'

'Bloody hell, Theo,' David raised his voice. 'If you're made this way, you go on being this way. If you are made half this way, you go on being half this way. If you're not made this way, you won't stop worrying about it.'

'You could go through your life as a queer? As a poof? As a pansy? And there's worse words than them for what it is.'

'Yeah yeah,' said David. 'And I've used 'em all, too. Bet we both have.'

'I won't be using them again,' said Theo. 'Not ever. Regardless of what happens to you'n'me.'

'You talk too much about it,' said David. 'You worry over it all the time. Just let things be as they are for as long as it is, well, for as long as it seems right. You haven't hurt me. Well, you have, really. You've had a go at killing me in your car and three-quarters killed me with your smoking. You know what? I can live with the rest. For now,' he looked at his friend, 'you can trust me.'

'Real, real funny,' said Theo. 'There are times when you seem years older'n me and you know it all. You! Kid from a little dump town you've never left and probably never will leave for long. Nice warm home and nice warm parents you love and, shit, you're not even awkward about saying you love them. Me? Whew! I been everywhere and sure done a heap of things you wouldn't dream of. At your age I got out of school. Cleared out. Escaped. Didn't know that, did you? Well, maybe you did. That's why I'm older'n the rest of you in our class and having to do now what I should have done then.'

'What did you do?'

'What d'you mean?'

'When you cleared out?'

'Mucked about. Took off for six months up in the islands on a charter yacht. I worked on it. God, I worked. That was the one thing told me that leaving school and nothing to show for it . .. guess that's part of why I'm here.'

'What about your mother?'

'What about her? She knew what I'd do.'

'Is she like her mother?'

'Like Gretel? I guess. They don't see much of each other and yet they are very close. Strange,' said Theo.

'How come?'

'God, you're the limit. I'm not going on about Mum and Gretel. You wanna know? You ask them.'

'Be a bit hard,' said David. 'Given I've never met your mother. I don't see why you need school, anyway.'

'What d'you mean?'

'Can't Gretel get you a good job in the hot-water bot-

73

tle place?'

'That's another thing about you,' said Theo. 'You never forget a word I say. Did you see my duck down on the pond?'

'Your duck?'

'Yes. My duck.'

'Just you remember, it's got to fly before you shoot it. Want me to send it up now? Get your gun.'

'No way,' said Theo. 'He's wounded. It's his wing, but I think he's getting better.'

'He's a her,' said David.

'I'm looking after him and I'm not gonna shoot him. I've fed it,' said Theo.

'Just don't give it the rest of that casserole,' said David. 'Unless you want it to sink.'

7

'What d'you see in him?' asked his cousin, Julie. 'I don't like him.' She had come to help with the preparations for David's birthday dinner. 'Just something about him I wouldn't trust. He's up himself. It's that look that says he thinks he's smarter, better than the rest of us. All the girls reckon that. D'you know he's not even asked any of us out?'

'Ho ho ho,' said David. 'I don't blame him. He's used to real women, not little kids. He told me. You should hear what he's done to some of them. What they've done to him, too. God . . .' he breathed. 'Yep. He told me all about it.'

'Go on,' said Julie, eagerly. 'Go on. Tell me. Come on.'

'No,' said David. 'Can't do that. He made me promise.'

'Oh yeah? I don't even think he's good looking.'

'I do,' said David, simply.

'You're not supposed to,' said Julie.

David knew he had reddened. 'Yeah. Well . . . I mean. He's okay, I guess.'

'Only good thing about him is his car. I'd go with him just for that,' said Julie, slicing banana into a bowl of fruit salad. 'And his weird mother. God, she's old. You seen her?'

'It's his granny and she's coming for dinner, so watch it. I'd sure go with her just for her car,' he said, and knew he'd unhooked himself. 'They're helluva rich. It's hot-water bottles.'

'Yes. I'd go with him, too, just for his money,' said Julie. 'Even though I don't like him.' She looked across at David. 'What about you, Davy? You haven't done much since Kathy left at the beginning of the year. The girls are only just all saying . . .'

'You can all mind your own business,' he laughed at her. 'I lead a very active private life that I keep hidden right away from you and your mates and for good reasons, too.'

'What? Round this dump?' she laughed at him. 'You! God, everyone knows about you and always has. You're sort of so open it's written all on your face. The girls all say you're just like a nice little trusting puppy.'

That's what you think, cousin. 'Yeah, yeah,' he put on a sorrowful look. 'Story of my life, eh? Woof. Woof. I'm just a dog.'

Maureen Mason enjoyed showing her garden to Gretel Meyer. 'It's not often anyone who knows any-thing about anything wants to have a really good look,' she said. 'I can't wait to see, Gretel, what it is you're doing on the old Norman property. David's told me so much.'

'You come any time,' said Gretel. 'Even if I am not there. David may bring you. He knows the garden quite well and, I must say, is quite a help.'

'He is. Of course, one day it will be his life.' His mother smiled. 'He does a lot here, too. The only boy in my living experience who really seems to enjoy mowing lawns. Do get him to help you.'

'I do. I do. A very willing worker,' said Gretel.

'I'm glad. His father is determined he shouldn't work at the shop this year. Exams and all that. Without his rugby he does have a little time. Make the most of it.' She smiled again.

'A boy to be proud of,' said Gretel. 'Now, tell me, my dear, magnolias. I see you have a collection.' She walked across the lawn. 'Lovely things. I hadn't known they did so well here. And what's this?' She bent.

Near the end of the meal David realised what was happening. Later, thinking back, he could spot that what was going on had been going on for at least an hour, longer even.

Their laughter was too loud. When he looked across at Theo he could see in his face the heightened colour, the glint in the eye that once, twice, he had seen before. Excitement. As for his cousin, well, there was no doubt in his mind as to what he could see there.

A pleasant meal. For the most part the adults chatted, ate, drank and kept to themselves. David, Theo and Julie looked after their own needs, helping themselves from the loaded table and sitting slightly apart from their elders. Because it was his party David felt he should, from time to time, join the grown-ups and it was at one of these times that he began to hear, and then to comprehend, what was going on between Theo and Julie.

And then, 'Just taking Julie out for a short drive. Okay? Wants to see what the car's like. You wanna come, David?'

Julie gave him no chance. 'Of course he doesn't. Anyway, he's gotta stay. It's his party.'

'Won't be long,' said Theo.

'We'll see about that,' said Julie, giggling.

David stayed. No option. No option on joining in with the adults. No option, either, but to control the sudden sickness, the near-nausea invading his gut.

The adults moved from the table. 'Come and sit over here, birthday boy,' his mother called from across the room and patted a place beside her on a sofa. 'Come on. What's happened to the other two?'

'Just gone out for a while.' He worked to steady his voice. 'Quick drive in Theo's car.'

'Not too quick, I hope,' said his aunt.

'She just wanted to see what it was like, Aunty Jan,' said David.

His uncle laughed. 'Grandson of yours is the answer to every young girl's dream, Gretel.'

'I think it might be the car rather than the grandson,' Gretel Meyer smiled. She looked closely at David. 'And you didn't go?' She smiled again.

'I just hope she puts on her seatbelt,' Julie's mother said, absently.

'You mustn't worry, dear. Theo is a good driver,' said Gretel.

David dragged himself back to the moment and wondered on what basis Gretel judged driving ability. 'Nothing to worry about, Aunty Jan,' he said.

'If he's half as good as this one here,' Jack Mason looked over at his son, 'he's a born natural. Drove since he was eight years old.'

'Nonsense,' said Maureen Mason.

'It's true, Mum,' said David. 'Just me 'n' Dad never told you.' He smiled at her. 'Used to take the shop van out on the old North road and Dad'd give me lessons.'

'Well, if he's half as good a driver as he is a gar-

78

dener,' said Gretel, 'it seems to me that he is most certainly a natural. A credit to you Jack, Maureen.'

His sister Janet telephoned. 'Happy birthday, Porky.' She used the nickname she had called him since the day he was born when, at age ten, she had considered he resembled nothing other than a small pig. 'Sorry I couldn't make it. Next year, I promise. When're you coming up to see me?'

'When you ask me,' he said, and looked at his watch. Thirty minutes.

'I'm asking you now, Porky. Come for a weekend. Now you're a big pig it's time Mum and Dad let you off the hook. Come when I've got a weekend off. Just ring when you can hitch a lift up or something.'

Forty minutes.

The soft chat of the adults did not deliberately shut him out. Rather, he chose not to join in and sat, still and quiet, among them.

'Hah! He does not believe me, this boy of yours, that come the spring I will have a lawn of blue.'

He got back into the talk. 'Well, I still reckon it's unlikely,' he said, shyly. 'Like, it's all flowers and when they die off it'll be one helluva mess.'

'For just a wee while,' said Gretel. 'Then, poof!' She expressed the point with a hand. 'I'll simply just mow it over with the rest of the lawn and wait till the next year. You'll see.'

'She, I mean Gretel, has got a white lilac. Never seen one of them before,' said David. 'Not white.'

'Not uncommon,' said Gretel.

'It's to remind her of her old home in Poland. They had one like it outside their house,' he forced himself to say, and knew that, now, he was talking too much. 'Outside her bedroom window. I said Gretel should go back to see it. Could still be there. But she's got no family there. Not now. Not even one, eh Gretel?'

'Not even one.' Gretel Meyer folded her hands.

'They all lived in this old, old house with cobblestones on the street outside just like a picture in a fairy story.' He looked at Gretel.

'How about coffee, Mother? Too much of that wine. Beer man, me.' Jack Mason stretched.

'How about coffee, Mother, indeed!' laughed his wife. 'David. Seeing your father wants coffee and seems to expect someone else to make it for him, come and give me a hand. Jan. Fred, and you too Gretel. Just stay put, the lot of you.'

Sixty minutes. One hour.

Seventy-two minutes.

They came in laughing and giggling and nudging at each other. 'This guy's sure some driver,' said Julie.

'Sure is,' said David. 'Did he get you to change a wheel for him?'

They ignored him and moved to the table to pour themselves coffee and then join the adults.

'I was beginning to think you two had got lost,' said Julie's mother. 'I hope for your sake, Theo, you didn't let her behind the wheel. You must have been gone for half-an-hour.'

'And now, young man,' said Gretel to Theo. 'It is time to take our leave. You've taken a young lady driving and now you may take an old lady home to bed.' She laughed her dry, harsh laugh. 'I do know how bad that sounds. No matter.'

A sick hate burnt inside him. It would not go away.

He thought he'd kill him. A nice, clean shooting accident and no one would ever guess. A loaded gun. An awkward fence. Boom!! Be a sort of enquiry, nothing more. And he, David, would be away, free. Had sure happened round these parts more than once. Nothing to it. David worked out the logistics.

Shooting would be best, even if it was too quick. Still, with a bit of thought and planning it needn't be all that quick. Not if everything was worked out real good before the event. Mind you, not too slow, either. Couldn't have anything suffer for too long. Not sporting. Mind you, there could be exceptions. Maybe just have him suffer long enough for him, Theo, to know what had hit him, who had hit him and why.

Without doubt shooting was the realistic way to go. Setting up a car accident was just too complicated, and why punish the poor car? And a fire and asphyxiation, what a lovely word, could just see fingers pointing the wrong way. No. Shotgun it would have to be. Better get in some cartridges with a heavier load. What might do for a duck might not do for Theo Meyer.

He lay on his bed. He lay in it. He got up and prowled his room. Back to the bed. In it.

Theo phoned. David would not take the calls. 'Tell him I'm too busy, Mum. I'm working. He knows that.'

David did work. Doggedly. Persistently.

Theo drove by the Mason house. Spotting the red car, David took off, over the back fence into a small patch of bush. 'He was here,' said Maureen Mason, puzzled. 'I don't know where he can have got to, Theo. Can I give him a message?'

Eventually Theo cornered David walking between town and home. There was no polite invitation. 'Get in the bloody car,' he called out loud. 'If you don't you just hang around and see what I yell out about you as loud as I can.'

David got in the car. Fast, too fast, Theo drove from the town. Neither of them spoke. Theo took the road out to the coast. Ten minutes, twenty, a half-hour, nothing said. The highway was minor, not busy. Theo crested the hill high above the coastline and drove into a deserted look-out. A popular summer picnic spot.

'Yeah yeah yeah,' said David. 'You can drive fast. So, what's new?' he sneered. 'Why the hell you dragged me out here?'

'What's crept into you?' asked Theo. 'As if I didn't know.' He lit a cigarette, opened the window and the outside cold blew in.

'It's cold,' said David.

'So? Suffocate then.' Theo closed the window.

'Why did you do it?' asked David, and try as he would he could not stop eyes prickling, filling, and tears rolling down his face. He shook his head angrily and turned his face from Theo.

'Dunno,' said Theo, sullen. 'Prove a point, I guess. Maybe she asked for it.'

'Asked for what?'

'Dunno.' Theo looked at David. 'If I had . . . I don't know. Yes, of course I know. There's a whole lot of reasons. You know that. First, well, she just wanted a ride in the car.'

'She got that all right.'

'Second, well, you pissed me off seriously.'

'I pissed you?' David sounded surprised. 'What'd I do?'

'Should catch yourself sometimes. Jesus! Bloody little saint. God, it was your birthday and we were there to give you a good time and what happens? You'd sit still for two frigging minutes then bounce up to check if the olds needed anything. You hardly got to eat a bloody thing. You . . . you . . .' He choked on the word. 'Too good to be true. Who the hell gives a stuff if Aunty's got an empty glass? Who cares? You do, that's who. You got right up my nose, mate. All she wanted was a ride in my car.' Flat.

'Yeah?'

'"Oh, he's such a lovely boy. Such a nice boy". That's what old ladies'd say about you. They'll still be bloody saying it when you're forty and dead. Sure won't say it about me.'

'You only took her for a ride?'

'No.'

Acid rose in David's throat. 'I could kill you.'

'I know you could,' said Theo. 'I know you could. I'd rather you didn't and I'm sorry.'

'She only wanted to try you on. Try you out or something.'

'I know that, too.'

'You let yourself be used, eh?' said David.

'Well, there are worse ways to be used,' said Theo.

'You make me sick,' said David.

'Look, kid.' Theo sounded desperate. 'I've told you, I've told you, I've told you . . . it's not all clear-cut like you want to make it. I'm struggling. Bloody struggling just to find out who I am. I haven't even started yet on *what* I am.'

'What about me?' asked David.

'What about you? I dunno. Look, if it's any comfort to you, all she wanted to talk about, well, not quite all, was about you and how lovely you are even if you are a bit thick.'

'I couldn't give a shit,' said David, and they sat in silence for a good two minutes. 'Give me a smoke?'

'Geddoff,' said Theo.

'Why not?'

'Nice boys don't. Think of Mummy and Daddy and Aunty and Uncle.' A little laugh. 'What would they think?'

'We can't solve it, eh?' said David. 'We just can't.' Then he smiled. 'Come on. Let's go down to the beach and we'll go for a run. Let me drive. Bet you let her drive.'

'If you want.'

'I was going to shoot you,' said David, before he started the car. 'Real slow.'

'You can't shoot slow,' said Theo. 'The bullets and shit come out quick.'

'I was going to shoot you so you'd croak real slow.'

'That's nice,' said Theo. 'Bloody nice. Don't need three guesses as to where I was gonna get shot. And I don't believe you, Mr Nice-Guy-Good-Sport. Would've been short, sharp and quick coming from you.'

'That's what you think,' said David, starting the car. He drove very quickly down the winding road to the beach.

The beach was deserted. A very grey day. It was not a swimming beach, not even a visiting beach. The surf was a hard pound, the rip was harder and the narrow strip of sand was as dirty a grey as the sky.

They ran for almost an hour. They didn't speak and ran apart for most of the time, intent on the rhythm of the run. Rain drizzled in and they ran on, pausing in stride only to jump hurdles of driftwood.

They came back and rested first, leaning, panting, heaving against the car. As the drizzle thickened into rain they got into the car and the interior fogged from the wet heat of their bodies.

'Better now?' asked Theo.

'Better'n what?'

'Than you were before,' said Theo.

'We should do more of it. It's good. Makes you feel alive.'

'I already know I'm alive,' said Theo. 'If you must know it makes me feel half dead. Are you all right?' he asked, softly, almost shyly.

'Yes. I'm all right. Let's go home. We'll go out for a shot if you like. There's time.'

'Good,' said Theo, but there was no enthusiasm. Then, 'No. I don't think I will.'

'Why not? Great weather. They'll be flying low.'

'Don't feel like it.' Theo was defensive.

'You sure?'

'Might as well tell you now,' said Theo, and he turned to look at David. 'I won't go again. I'm sorry.'

'That's cool,' said David. 'It's okay.'

'Yeah. That's it. It's okay for you.' Theo deliberately mistook David's reply. 'Not okay for me.'

'Thought you enjoyed it.'

Theo looked at David again. 'When I get out there I want to kill. When I get home I feel different. I feel sad. You'd never understand and I'm not going to try and make you. Guess I'm not a hunter after all.'

After a moment or two David said, 'It's all right, Theo. It's all right.'

'I'm not gonna go on about it,' said Theo.

'No need to,' said David, then he laughed. 'That duck at the bottom of your garden must've known something, must've had a good talk to you.'

'Something like that,' said Theo. 'It's also a little bit

about what's good for you doesn't have to be good for me. Let's leave it, eh? One thing, though.' He grinned at David.

'What's that?'

'You're right about these long runs. You do feel good after one. Let's do it again.'

'Not right now,' said David, quickly.

'I wasn't suggesting right now, thicko.'

'Yeah. Well, they're supposed to be good for getting rid of our sex urges. Old Bob Green, our coach, said that. Or something like that.'

'Bugger can speak for himself. Let's go,' said Theo.

8

May sifted wet into June and June dragged, colder and wetter yet, into July. Slow days. School dragged even slower. For the first time David began to have doubts as to the wisdom of his giving up rugby. If nothing else, at least the game had been a good time-filler. Had given, too, a series of highs and highlights to the very worst months of the year.

When a bout of 'flu hit hard at school he allowed himself to be talked into playing a couple of games. He enjoyed it.

'Next season, Davy?' said the coach.

'We'll see, Mr Green. I dunno,' said David.

His father's joy knew no bounds. 'It's in your blood, boy! It's in your blood!'

At least he was fit. Theo had seen to that. The two of them now ran three, four times a week. It had become a pattern. They set out regardless of the weather and, dogged, would run for a good hour, coming back to the Meyer house, showering together, dressing and then, seldom speaking, settling to an hour or more of study.

'Gonna give a party,' said Theo, on one such evening. 'Gretel's in Auckland for three days.'

'What? To make more hot-water bottles?'

'You don't let anything rest, kid. Gretel does not make hot-water bottles and never has. Use your brain. Bottom dropped out of the hot-water bottle market when we all got into electric blankets. If you must know, she goes up to see her stockbroker and her accountant. She owns a slice of a firm that makes rubber stuff. God knows if they still make hot-water bottles. She's on the board of the company and she goes to meetings. Satisfied?'

'Hmmm . . . What about . . .?'

'Any more you want to know, ask Grandmama. Oh, yeah. They do condoms, too.' Theo grinned. 'If you ever want any . . . How about this party?'

'Dunno.' David was none too sure. 'I don't know.'

'I'd behave myself,' said Theo. 'Promise I would.'

'I wasn't thinking about that,' David lied. 'Just that I reckon parties around here aren't much like what you'd be used to.'

'How come?'

'Like, well . . . see, even if it was snowing a good half of the guys'd end up chucked in your duck pond. They'd drink anything that's going and you couldn't stop them and . . .' He looked and sounded even more uncertain.

'Doesn't sound anything different from what I've been used to,' said Theo.

'It's a pity you can't cook,' said David.

'I can so cook,' said Theo.

'No you can't,' said David.

'So, why's it a pity?'

'You could sort of just invite six or eight or so for a meal rather than a full-on party. You can still have booze.'

'Sounds okay.'

'But you can't cook.'

88

'I could cook enough for that,' said Theo. 'I know I could. I bet you'd help. Cousin Julie could help, too.' He threw up his hands. 'Don't shoot me! Please!'

David ignored him for a moment. 'Yeah. That might work. Me'n'Julie and you could get it all ready. Invite another half dozen. Whoever you like. Then you wouldn't have twenty or thirty bloody hoons wrecking Gretel's house. Even so, bet there'd be a pile of mess. Have you asked Gretel?'

'Not yet.'

'I think you better.'

Julie couldn't wait to get started. Gretel was agreeable. 'Just so long as I don't have to do the cooking before I go or the dishes when I return,' she said. Not a word about looking after the place, looking after her things. Not a word about someone older to keep things in order. 'I will be bringing back with me, or having sent back, an order of trees for that top bank. In return for using my food, and just a tiny wee drop of my wine, I expect the two of you to dig holes for me to plant them in. Right?'

'What are you getting?' David was interested.

Theo sighed.

'A few of the smaller things. I want to start filling in a few of the gaps between the big ones. Any ideas?' She smiled at David.

'Conifers,' said David, firmly. 'They do well round here. A lot you could get. Most of what you've planted, already, lose their leaves. Conifers don't. You can get all colours, all sizes. Get 'em to tone in with what you've already got. You know all that, anyway.'

Theo rolled his eyes.

'Yes, yes, yes. I do know. But I do like to hear you tell me,' she laughed at him.

'Gold ones. Bronzey ones and a few blues. A couple of blue cedars. They're very lovely,' said David.

Theo moaned.

'You and your trees. If your father has some, put them aside for me. I'll trust your judgment.' Gretel laughed again.

'Just remember how slow they grow,' said David. 'Blue ones'd look lovely up near your blue lawn and Dad has got two or three.'

Theo groaned.

'Six weeks and it'll be a blue lawn. You mark my words,' said Gretel. 'And you keep an eye on my bad grandson, here. No nonsense at his dinner party. Dinner party! Hah! That I should see the day. I just hope that nice little cousin of yours, the one who made the lambs' eyes at you at your birthday . . . well, I just hope she can cook.'

'See!' Theo was triumphant. 'I was right. And it's sheep's eyes, Grandmama, and if either of you mention another bloody tree I'll take me shotgun and go out and blast every bugger you've planted. And that won't be blood sport, it'll be sap sport and a helluva lot of fun.'

'I told you I could do it,' said Theo. Only David was left with him, stacking the last of the glassware and plates into the dishwasher.

'You! You could do it? Me'n'Julie did it.'

'I opened bottles and stuff. I peeled potatoes.'

'Great, mate.'

There hadn't been too much mess and even the noise level was moderate. As the term was drawing to its close, most of the talk had been about exams, chances, opportunities or lack of them. The first signs of winter thinning brought out talk of summer and sun. They played music and some of them danced. Mostly they talked and when they weren't talking they ate and drank.

'You could stay,' said Theo.

'I don't think I could,' said David.

'Why not?'

'No. No, I can't stay.'

'Please stay,' said Theo.

'Look, I'll be out tomorrow. We'll go for a run. Then we've got to dig those holes for Gretel,' said David.

'Stay tonight. Please, David.'

David looked at Theo. He looked away. He breathed deeply. At last he said, 'All right. I'll stay.'

Theo said nothing for a while and then, 'Better ring Mummy, hadn't you?'

'It's all right. I told them I wouldn't be home,' said David.

'I could kill you,' said Theo.

'I wasn't sure. That's all.' David stood and looked down at Theo. 'Come on,' he said. 'I'm stuffed. Let's go to bed.'

They went to bed and, curled in each other's arms, they slept.

'No, boy. Over there. To the right. A bit further. Now dig!'

David dug until he felt his back was breaking. When Gretel Meyer went to buy trees she bought them in bulk.

'Now, then. I think those little flaxes should be at the foot of the bank, not halfway up. Dig them out,

David.'

He dug again.

'Boring, Granny. Time for a break,' called Theo.

'Are you staying for dinner, David?' Gretel asked.

'Ah, well, dunno if I . . . dunno about Mum.'

'Your mother is bringing the dinner. She telephoned earlier. She knew it was planting time and she kindly offered,' said Gretel.

The seed of a friendship had been sown. The common bond of a love of plants and gardening is a sound link. 'Great. Fine. I didn't know,' said David.

'Damn,' said Theo. 'And I could've cooked. Getting right into this cooking.'

'It could only be better than your gardening, Theodore. Your ability, I mean,' said his grandmother. 'Now, dig.'

'White lilac's sure budding great now, Gretel,' said David after they had eaten.

She looked at him for a moment and it was almost as if he wasn't there. Then she started to speak. Slowly at first and very softly. Gretel sat at the end of the kitchen table, the surface of the table littered with what they hadn't eaten. 'I was younger than you when last I saw it. The white lilac. What was I? Twelve? Fourteen? I don't remember.' She whistled tunelessly for a moment. 'At first it was if it would never happen. As if it could never happen. Why, in the name of God, should it happen? We had lived, my family, in that town for hundreds of years. For centuries. Beyond all belief. Safe? We were so safe. Huh! As safe as a stupid chicken with the axe above its head. And all our friends? Our dear friends, our neighbours . . . they saw it could never happen . . . what we heard was happening to others . . . couldn't happen to us . . .

'One early summer morning. I smell the scent of that lilac until this day. What did I know of what it was all about? My aunt, my great-aunt Esther, she says to me "Pack your clothes, my little one. You are going away. By yourself," she says. "Don't ask me. Don't cry. Don't ask."

'Going away? For why? What about my school? A good school, our school, and me so bright I could beat them all. My friends? What about my friends? What . . . what about my father and my Hannah and my Sarah? What about . . .?'

No one interrupted. Maureen Mason looked down at the table. She knew what could, what would come. David did not know, but rather sensed that at the core, at the centre of what she was saying, there would be little that was good. Theo smoked. He leaned back in his chair, eyes almost closed, very still.

'Father took me to the granary. "Don't talk," he said. "Don't ask." What was I to think? How was I to know that in the minutes, the hours, the days, the weeks, the months surrounding this very moment, what was happening to me was happening to millions? He took me to the place where the lilac bloomed and he put in my hands a small purse, a little leather pouch. "Should God will," he said to me, "one day you will come back. If God wills maybe you will still find it here." And he took the pouch from my hand and dug into the soil, the dirt at the back of the lilac bush, and he buried that purse. He kissed me. My aunt Esther kissed me. My sisters? I do not know where they were. To this day I do not know where they were. I never saw them again. I . . . never . . . saw . . . any . . . of . . . them . . . again . . .'

'Gretel.' Maureen Mason spoke and touched lightly on the arm of the old woman. 'If you don't want to . . . If it's too . . .'

Gretel Meyer continued as if the other had not spoken. 'Father said to me, "They will be good to you. For years I have taken their grain and my father before and never did they get the bad price, not even when . . ." Pah!' She turned her head in a look of distaste and then spat on the floor. 'He should have killed me. He should have killed me as I stood beneath that lilac and let my blood feed that plant.'

With a shaking hand she poured, slopped, wine into her glass. She held the bottle out to the Masons. 'Yes, I survived. Of course I did. I am here. One year, two with these good people we had paid so much for their grain. One year, two, with these such good friends. Friends!' She spat again as she said the word. 'I lived, if you call it living, out in the cow barn with the cow. The only kindly sound I was to hear for those years was the moo of that cow. Until they ate her. I was the slave for them and, dear God, how I worked and little more than a child. But I knew now what was happening. They told me, these good friends. How they told me. So often they told me and they laughed at me as they told me "Fuel for the ovens," is what they called me. "Only good Jew is a dead Jew," is what they told me. But they fed me. Not much, mind. Enough so that I could work, I could carry, lift, dig and, when I had finished for the day, lie back for them. Three of them. The man and his two sons, one fourteen and one sixteen, something like that. God, let them burn in the fires of hell for what they did to me. For what they did to a child. Child?' A bark of laughter. 'I was not a child for long.' Gretel Meyer raised her eyes and looked, absently almost, at Maureen Mason. 'A living hell, and yet it was not until much later that I learnt others had it worse. At least I was warm by that old cow and it would likely have gone on except . . .'

She drank again.

The spell of her story cast a web of silence over her audience. the three, Maureen, David and Theo, were still. The woman drank and then continued. 'I was so very stupid. I should have counted my blessings and put up with it all. One day I couldn't. The younger one came to me in the night and took me. I could not bear it one moment longer. I bit him.' A savage cheerless joy crossed her eyes. 'I bit that pig for all I was worth and I will not tell you where I bit. Ha! Kosher? I think not. I bit until my teeth met and I still hear the sound of that scream . . . it is good.

'Silly little Gretel. "There is a Jew dog in our barn. Get her!" Ah, the frying pan and the fire. The frying pan and the inferno, the furnace! They got me.'

'Gretel,' said Maureen Mason. 'I think . . .'

'It is all right. It is good and right and it is the mo-ment,' said Gretel. 'It is not often I . . . Better, now, that I finish. My dear father, he was right. He did save me. It was 1944 and the Russians not far. At least I had some food and I was better fodder for a factory than a gas chamber. I went to the camps. Ah, yes. To Treblinka and then to Sobibor where most were nearer death than me and who died, day by day, right there in front of me and just skin and just bone. It was there that I said to myself I would live. I could work. I did work. Those who did not work died. There is nothing mystic about death. One moment you live, are alive. A puff of wind, of any-thing at all, and then, like a leaf from a tree in autumn, you fall. Simple.

'As you see, I did not die. I will not tell you the small horrors, the big horrors I saw. The end? The beginning? It came. I marched out, skin and bone and not much more. But I was alive.'

Slowly she rolled up the sleeve of her shirt. She turned her wrist to them and they looked. While the years had blurred the outlines of the tattooed series of numbers and while they could not all be read, the message of the whole was fully clear.

'I want to cry,' said Maureen Mason, very quietly. 'I want to cry but I think my tears would insult you.'

Gretel Meyer said nothing for a moment or two. She fingered her wrist and looked down at the label. 'Nothing hurt more than this. Not the beatings, the threat of death, the stench and stink of death. Nothing has ever hurt more inside me than the little sting pricks of this marking.' She laughed and the sound shocked Maureen and David Mason. 'It is human nature. The best and the worst. So funny, now. This horrible thing I wear with pride. I have served my time, it says. Ah, me.' She paused. 'I do believe that enough is enough. One day, maybe, there is more. But only the fullstops, really.'

'We should go, David,' said his mother.

'What nonsense,' said Gretel Meyer. 'I have given him a good lesson in history. It surprises me how quickly it becomes just that. No more than "Once upon a time" . . . Besides,' and she continued to shake herself back into the here and now, 'these two young men of ours, Maureen, have still to do the dishes and to make their olders a cup of coffee which you and I, Maureen, shall drink with a little something much stronger. Let us go through, my dear. These two may wait on us.'

'Why didn't you ever tell me?' David asked Theo as they made coffee. 'Why? Like I've heard of the Jews

96

and what happened but . . .'

'We've been around for a long long time, kid. We're still around in spite of the devils, in spite of the mad men.'

'Why didn't you tell me?'

'It wasn't for me to tell,' said Theo. He made the coffee while David tidied the dinner mess. They went through to the two women, poured the coffee and then went out to Theo's room. 'Least you can understand why she doesn't bother much about stupid junk like whether I smoke or have one drink too many. Not even the fast driving, and she sure can't talk about that.'

'Doesn't what she said mean much to you?'

'Mean much?' Theo was angry. 'What the hell d'you mean? It is me. That is what I am. She is what I am. That, and more besides. Stuff she hasn't told you, might never tell you.'

'Like what?'

'Like shut up, David.' Theo turned from him.

David crossed the room to him. 'Hey. I didn't mean . . . I didn't. Just, well, I don't know.'

Theo turned to him. 'No, man. I know you didn't. See, I know her story word for word. I know it. But I don't hear it from her lips very often. She is what I am,' he cried.

David held Theo in his arms and did what he could to comfort his friend.

'Shit,' said Theo, forcing a laugh and pulling free of David, 'let's talk about now and not about then.' But he couldn't leave the essence of what they had just heard. 'Reckon you can see, too, why food and cooking doesn't mean too much to the old girl. Just so long as there's enough of it and it fills your guts. Doubt she ever tastes it. Eating has got only one dimension for

Gretel, that's what Mum says. One purpose. You get it in. You keep it down. You stay alive. Do you know why she wrecks one Porsche after another?'

'No.'

Theo laughed. 'It's the one thing with her that has no logic at all. She says that treating them like shit is the one way she's got of getting back at the fuckin' Nazi bastards. Just think about that.'

9

'If I work all over Christmas, Dad, reckon I'll have enough to get something reasonable. Like, well, with what I've saved already,' said David.

'Why, David? Why?' asked his mother. 'You can use my old car if you need to. You know that. Apart from anything else, you couldn't afford to keep one of your own on the road.'

'I've worked it out. I can,' he said, flatly.

'There's no need . . .' She shrugged, recognising the battle was pointless.

'On your own head be it,' said Jack Mason.

'And that's just where I don't want it to be,' said his wife. 'It'll be some clapped-out old banger.'

David grinned at her. 'Worried what it'll look like in the drive, eh Mum? Worried what the neighbours'll say? All right. I'll settle for a whatsit, a compromise. You buy me one like what Theo's got.'

'Dream on, son,' said his father. 'The day I can afford to spoil you rotten . . .'

'Theo's not spoilt,' said David.

'Maybe. Maybe not,' said Maureen Mason. 'But he's certainly not from quite the same sort of background you're used to.'

'Maybe Dad should've started a hot-water bottle factory,' said David. 'Seems to help.'

'That's as may be,' said his mother. 'Whatever Gretel Meyer has ended up with now seems to have been paid for, well and truly, along the way.' She said nothing for a moment. 'Poor, poor soul.'

'She might be a lot of things but she sure ain't poor,' said David.

'Pour soul,' Maureen Mason repeated.

David looked at his mother. 'You know what she told us, Mum? Just how the hell could one lot of people have done that load of shit to another lot of people? I know it was a long time ago, but . . .'

Jack Mason stood. 'You blind or something, son? Deaf? Look at the telly any bloody night. They're still bloody doing it!'

'Yeah, yeah. I know. Just that I don't understand it. I wonder what else happened to Gretel. I wonder,' said David.

Maureen Mason smiled at her son. 'Well, love. Maybe she'll tell us, maybe she won't. Don't ask. Don't try asking. She'll tell us, if ever, in her own good time.'

From the sharp claws of winter to a wickedly false warm spring in mid-August. No one thought it would last. Everyone made the most of it. As an added bonus the warm weather coincided with the school holidays.

'I wanna do a real long run,' said Theo. 'Like, let's hitch a ride up into those hills where we got to when we ended up in that ditch. Right up the top, further even. Then we'll run back. How about it?'

'Fine by me,' said David. 'You sure you're up to it?'

'Me? Don't you worry about me, kid. Anyway. We

don't have to bust a gut. We'll take it easy. Have a few breaks. We get back, eat and then work a bit on the stuffing maths. We need it, both of us. What d'you reckon?'

'Sounds good.'

'Stay the night?'

'Sure.'

'Gretel's away. Think she gets back tomorrow.'

'Burgers, then?'

'All right by me,' said Theo.

It took until mid-afternoon to thumb a lift on a forestry truck. 'You guys are mad,' said the driver. 'All that way? Bloody mad. Sure beats me how you fitness freaks get your kicks.' He patted a fat belly. 'As long as me elbow's in form that's all I worry about.'

They laughed with him.

They ran. At times they kept to the rutted form of the roadway. At other times David led them, ducking and diving into scrub, along half-formed goat tracks and through stands of pine. The light was clear and the sun played on the trees, shooting beams of light through branches onto the muddied, brown-pooled paths. When they could they settled into a rhythmic jog and solidly, surely ate into the distance. As they always did they ran apart. As they ran the sun set into a flamed horizon, the vivid colours of which told that the fine warm spell might be drawing to an end. Dusk fell. They stopped for a break, for a drink and a barley sugar. 'Still gotta way to go,' said David. 'You gonna make it?'

'No sweat,' Theo laughed. 'Not much option, eh?'

'Yeah. Well, we can cross-country most of the rest of it. I know the way. By the time it's dark we'll be back on the last road. Sure you're okay?'

'Yes, Mother,' said Theo. 'Surprise even myself. Just wish I'd brought me smokes.' He took a side-long look at David.

'I don't believe it,' said David.

'Knew I'd get a bite,' said Theo. 'Come on.'

In the last of the dusky light they came out onto a side road and wearily pounded the remaining distance to the Meyer house. They slumped, fully exhausted, onto the kitchen floor. Three, five, seven minutes and neither spoke.

They drank. 'Reckon we done us a marathon?' asked Theo, wiping his mouth and missing most of the trickle of juice that ran down his chin and onto his chest. 'I reckon we done a marathon.'

'Just about. Dunno. What've we done? Three, four hours? Yeah. We could've,' said David.

'Christ, I'm hot. Let's shower.'

'Yeah. In a minute,' said David.

They drank more and slowly recovered to a pleasantly exhausted half-life. They showered. Hot. Cold. Hot again. They gave themselves up to the easing sharpness of the jets of water. They ate. Too tired to go for burgers, they picked at the ill-assorted selection in Gretel's fridge. Drank more.

'God, I'm stuffed,' said David.

'Maths is, too. I'm too tired to work,' said Theo. 'Let's go to bed.'

They lay, side by side, on Theo's bed. They talked, just a very little. Weary and warm, both. Soon the talk stopped and, slowly, they drowsed their way into a full, deep sleep. Some time in the night, the warmth of the heated room and of their close bodies caused them to shrug off bathrobes and they lay, near-naked, fast asleep, together, holding, half-entwined.

Towards very early morning, Gretel Meyer came back from Auckland. Tired, she smiled slightly and followed a trail of discarded clothing and open doors to the light still burning in her grandson's room. She stood in the doorway. She looked.

'Ah, God,' she whispered to herself and then raised a finger to her lips. She half-turned to leave the room, but then turned back. She picked up the duvet from the floor. Gently she covered the sleeping boys. Very, very softly she kissed the head of each and stood back. 'So beautiful,' she said and, turning, she left the room.

'I came in so late,' said Gretel. 'I hope I didn't wake you. I felt like driving late at night.'

'Heard nothing,' said Theo. 'Too tired. We went for this marathon run. Just about one, we reckon. Too tired even to eat much when we got back. Reckon we could just about do a horse right now, eh David?'

'Sure could. Well, half a one.'

'Make yourselves what you will,' said Gretel. 'There are a few things I need to see to, calls to make. Then I must go into town. Will you be staying tonight, David?'

'Can't. Promised Dad two days of very hard labour. Need the cash, see. It's for my car fund.'

'Good. Good.' She smiled. 'This Theo, here, just might have one or two days of hard labour for which I shall pay him absolutely nothing at all.'

'Aw, gee, Granny,' said Theo.

It was three days of hard labour. Three days before David had a chance to bike out to the Meyer house.

It rained. Again it was cold.

'Ah, David. Come in. I have made coffee. We shall have some.' Gretel held open the door.

'Just thought I'd see Theo. Haven't had a chance. You got no idea how hard Dad made me work for just a little bit of pay. This rate and I'll be sixty before I get a car. He's doing it on purpose.'

'Come in, my dear. Quick. It is so cold.' She led him through to the kitchen.

A premonition. 'Where's Theo?' And then he knew.

'Theo has gone,' said Gretel.

'Gone? What do you mean, gone?'

'He has gone back to Auckland, my dear. His mother returned. It was sooner than we thought.'

'What about school?' Stupid question.

'School? Why? He will simply return to his school there.'

'Why?'

'Sit down, my dear,' She touched him and with that touch David knew that she knew.

He shrugged her off. 'I don't want to sit down. Gone? He never said nothing, anything, to me.' He moved to the other side of the kitchen table, away from the woman. Anger tore into him and at him, but he didn't rage. David spoke very quietly. 'You know. I know you know. You know about us, about him and me, eh?' He breathed hard. 'We never did no harm. We never did anything wrong and it's not wrong, it isn't. You know about him'n'me, eh? And you got rid of him.'

'My dear. My dear.' She spoke as quietly as he did. 'It is better . . . better . . .'

'Better? Better for who?' He stood away from the table and he spoke at Gretel Meyer through clenched teeth. 'I'm going now. I won't ever come here again. Not ever. I don't care what happens to your bloody blue lawn. And I do not care about your lilac bush.'

104

10

A month. 'I've never seen you work this hard,' said his mother. 'You've got to get out more, dear. Are you missing Theo?'

'Missing who?' he said, and got back to work.

Not a word. Nothing. He worked.

'Guess who I've had a letter from?' said his cousin Julie. 'From Theo Meyer, that's who.' She didn't wait for him to guess.

'So? What's he say?' He forced himself.

'Oh, just all about how his mother came back from wherever she was, all unexpected and that. He says for me to keep a good eye on you.'

'Does he?'

'Sure. Here.' She held out the letter. 'Read it for yourself.'

He knew his hand trembled as he took the letter. He forced his eyes down onto the familiar handwriting. Kept them there. Took in the only thing that interested him — the address at the top of the page.

Why waste time? 'Got two days' study leave, Mum. This Friday, next Monday. I sure as hell don't need to study, you know that. I want to go up to Auckland and stay with Janet. Can I?'

'May you,' the teacher corrected. 'It's all right with me, love. Better make sure it's all right with her. Dad and me certainly can't come. You'll have to catch the bus.' She tousled his head. 'Actually, I think it's a lovely idea. The two of you have never seen enough of each other. Guess you'd better blame Dad and me for that. Having you ten years apart might have something to do with it. Anyway, the break'll do you good. Even if Jan's working, I'm sure you'd enjoy a poke around the city by yourself. I know I do. It's time you got away out on your own for a while.'

'Whew! You do go on, Mum. I'm not leaving home, you know,' David laughed at her.

His sister met him.

'Porky! You're taller than ever. Have you grown half a head since I last saw you? You're sure looking down on me these days.'

'That wouldn't be hard, short-arse,' he said.

'Cheeky little beggar!'

He knew her flat. 'You'll have to sleep on the sofa. Just for tonight. Don't blame me if your feet hang over the end. You can use Carol's room from tomorrow.' She was referring to her flatmate. 'She's away for a few days. You know I've gotta work. I'm off tomorrow morning. You can take me out to lunch and we'll have a good old pig-out, Porky.'

He pulled a face at her. 'Aw, gee. I'm not made of money.'

'Mean little devil. You're loaded. Mum told me.'

'It's for my car,' he said.

'You can just put up with spending a bit of it on me first,' said Janet. 'Carol and me are taking you out to eat tonight and I'm going to buy you something to wear. Call it a late birthday present.' She looked at him. 'Yes.

106

Yes. Something a bit trendier than Mum'd ever get you.'

'You got a map of the city?' he asked.

'Sure. Somewhere around. Why?'

'Oh, nothing. Just if you're working and I want to find my own way around when you've lent me your car to drive.'

'Piss off, blossom. You can take a bus,' said his sister. She gave him a big hug. 'Nice to see you, little one.' She punched his arm.

She bought him clothes. She fussed over him. He lapped it all up. With Carol, her flatmate, they ate their way through a good number of the dishes at an Indian restaurant.

'What's on your mind, Piglet?' She pretended to tuck him in, later that night. 'If you want to talk about something, anything, you just fire away. It's not Mum and Dad?'

'Course not. They're fine. You're imagining things,' he said.

'If you say so,' said Janet. 'Better get to sleep then. Don't have too many nightmares about how much my lunch tomorrow will cost you.' She gave him a quick kiss.

He dressed in his new gear again and spent some time admiring his image in the mirror. Sister and brother browsed around the shops in the Saturday morning hustle and bustle. He took her to lunch. 'Look, Janet,' he said. 'Eat what you like. Eat as much as you like. You can always start your diet tomorrow. Be my guest.'

'Diet? Diet? I've never been on a diet in all my life.' Almost a squawk. 'Diet? What're you talking about?'

'Oh, I am sorry. I just thought you said,' David giggled. 'Did you say you had a boyfriend at the moment?'

'You . . .'

'Just could be because men go for rather smaller women than what you are,' he said, forcing himself to keep a very straight face. 'Don't you get me wrong, Jan. I'm not saying . . .'

'You little swine! Pig!' She laughed very loudly as she spoke and heads turned towards them from several tables. 'I think I'll just have a tomato and a lettuce leaf,' she said to the waiter. 'And my little boy's having nothing.'

They talked through lunch until it was time for her to leave for work. They talked of home and school and friends and family and most of David relaxed. 'You've got the key. I won't be in till late. There's plenty to eat and you've got the telly,' she said.

'I don't eat tellies,' he eyed her. 'You might. I don't.'

'I'll shove it down your throat if you're not careful. Then I'll give you an enema, make sure it goes right through,' said Janet.

'What's an enema, Mummy?' he asked, quite loudly.

'If you don't know now, dear, just let it be a pleasant surprise,' said his sister. 'You know how to get home?'

'Stop worrying, woman. I've got the map. I've got my mouth. I can always ask.'

'I'm off,' said Janet. 'Finish my dessert if you like. I've hardly touched it.'

He ate what was left of their food and then took out his map and checked again. Simple. No more than three or four blocks up and a couple of streets down. He looked at his watch, ordered another cup of coffee, drank it and then paid for their meal.

It was a bit further than the map had shown, but still not too far. Good walking distance. The streets were tree-lined, the buildings old and the traffic noise every-where. It was an old house. Three floors, three flats. A small, low-fenced garden outside. David checked name-plates. Meyer. Second floor. He climbed the stairs two at a time and stood in front of a red-painted door on a small, carpeted landing. Meyer. It said so.

He pressed the bell. Nothing. Pressed again. No re-sponse. Knocked on the door. Still nothing. Again, more urgently. There was no one home.

Why hadn't he thought of this? This wasn't part of the picture. No one home? David stepped back and considered the door. Puzzled. No part of his plan, this.

There was nothing else he could do. He went back down the stairs, out the front door and onto the pave-ment. He looked up and down the footpath. No one. He sat down on the garden wall and waited. Five minutes. Ten. He would wait. Yes. This was what he would do. Just wait. Everyone's got to return to base, to burrow, at some time. Even Theo Meyer. Could he have gone down to Gretel's? Even now was he knocking on his, David's, own front door? No matter. He'd still wait. An hour? A day? How long?

The sun served to sooth and he leaned back into the dense growth of a couple of shrubs. Half-an-hour. No one went in or out of the building. Forty minutes. One or two doubts. Sure was a long time, forty minutes. David stood and looked about him. Looked up an down the street.

Then he saw him. He saw Theo. His heart jumped, lurched. The pulse in his neck pounded. He wanted to run. To him? Away from him? He shrank back into the growth of the tree. Theo was not alone. He walked with a girl. A girl? The two of them stopped, half a dozen houses away. They talked. Saying goodbyes? David could see them speak but not hear what was spoken. He heard them both laugh and each waved to the other as they parted.

Theo broke into a jog and that familiar sight caused another lurch in David's chest. A slow pantomime of a jog. Seemed minutes. Was really seconds. Theo saw David and stopped. Stood stock still. 'It's you!'

David said nothing.

'What . . . what are you doing here?'

'I had to come.'

They faced each other. Very close. Their eyes did not meet and it seemed that each looked, stared into the distance, the space beyond the other. 'Come inside,' said Theo. He led the way.

A pigsty of a place. Drink cans, glasses, ashtrays, books, cassettes, clothes clean and dirty, a jumbled chaos. 'Don't mind the mess,' said Theo. 'Mum's doing some conference down south. Away till next week.' Then he risked a smile at David. 'Reckon I should spot a couple of aprons? Wanna drink?' He hardly paused. 'Here.' He tossed a can of Coke. 'Clear a chair. Sit down.'

David just stood. He saw nothing of the room. His eyes stayed on Theo.

'Mum's as untidy as me. Make a good pair, her'n'me.' He tried a smile. 'I'll get it a bit straight for when she gets back.'

David went on standing and he breathed heavily and slowly.

'For Christ sake, say something.' Theo couldn't stand the silence. 'Why've you come?'

'Why did you go?'

'You know why I went.'

'You didn't have to.'

'I had no option. None at all.' Theo sat, drank, bent

his head and stared at the floor.

'I miss you,' said David.

'Me, too,' said Theo.

'What did we do? What did we ever do? God, now, well, I just wish we'd done everything I ever wanted to do. What'd we do? Sweet fuckin' nuthin', that's what. Well.' David looked hard at Theo. 'I just wish we'd done it all.'

'So do I,' said Theo.

'Why did she, Gretel, send you away? What'd she think? God, I hate her,' said David.

'I don't,' said Theo. 'You don't, either. You don't know. All she said was that she knew what was happening and she thought it would be right if I came back here and Mum was back and all that.'

'She should have kept her nose out of our business,' said David.

'She said she knew how much we cared about each other. She said that was good. Look, David, never, ever did she say anything about anything being right or wrong. She didn't. She said maybe we had got too close, too quickly, and it was time to give it a rest, a break. She said, and I guess I can't argue with her on this one, that she was too old to take the responsibility.'

David yelled at him. 'It's not that she had to do anything. She didn't have to do squat! We had done it all ourselves. Why didn't you come and tell me? Why? Why didn't you write? Why? Didn't I mean anything? Was I just a nothing?'

'You know why,' said Theo. 'This, all this, is why. I was scared. Scared of what I might do. Sure as fuck scared of what you might do. It seemed best.'

'Best for bloody who?'

They sat in silence. Theo played with his empty drink

111

can, twisting it, forcing it from shape. David stared out of the window.

'You got part of it wrong,' said Theo, eventually. 'I wasn't going away for ever. Gretel even said make it three or four months and then, if I wanted, come down again for weekends, whatever. I was going to do just that.'

'Fine, fine, fine,' said David. 'You might've told me. I never knew none of that.'

'Gretel . . .' began Theo.

David interjected. 'I haven't seen her and I don't want to.'

'She'll be missing you,' said Theo.

'Couldn't care less,' said David.

'I will do that. Come down again, I mean,' said Theo. 'Look, kid, all of me misses you. There's not much of any day or night when you're not in my head, one way or another. I see you running. I see you shooting. I see you in Granny's garden. I hear you, God how I hear you, bloody arguing every bloody point with me. I don't know how I see you. I don't know whether I see you as a friend. As a brother. As a lover. I don't know if what I feel is just because we got so close and spent so much time together. Don't you dare think it's only you who has feelings. Don't you blame me for not getting in touch with you. Do you ever think what it might have been like for me if I had done just that? You said to me, way back once, that you'n'me were different. You said I felt for you as well as for myself. Then you said you just felt for yourself. You did, David. You did. God knows, maybe we do need a bit of time apart so's we can see what our feelings really are and what it is we really are.'

'Oh, I see,' said David. 'I get it. What you're saying is

that it'd be a good idea to wait and see how I feel when the next new guy comes to town. Is that it? That's a load of crap and you know it. You should listen more to your grandma, Theo. What you're saying is that it's probably okay if we find out we fit one sort of label. Testing yourself already, Theo? Eh? Saw you with that girl.'

'Oh, stick it, kid. She'n'me went to kindergarten together.' Theo sounded impatient. 'Why don't you hit me?'

'What the hell?'

'Least I understand that. Least your violence is black and white,' he laughed. 'Anyway. How did you get up here? Staying anywhere? Let's get onto something simple.'

They both stood. They looked at each other. They came together and for two, three minutes they held each other. Very still. When they parted, Theo said to David, 'Better?'

'Bit better than when I came,' said David.

They spent the rest of the afternoon together and in the early evening Theo got his car and they drove in the city, out of the city. They talked and they laughed, even. They stopped at a beach and ate fish and chips and then drove some more. They drove back to David's sister's flat. When she came in from the hospital they were still there, eating toast and drinking beer. 'Jan. This is Theo Meyer. He was . . .'

'I know. Don't tell me. It's your grandmother who's built the first new place in town since the first settlers,' she laughed. 'Mum's told me. You live up here?'

'Yeah,' said Theo. 'Met David when I was down with my grandmother for a couple of terms. Funny as.' He pointed at David. 'Just bumped into each other in the

113

city.'

'Long arm of coincidence, eh?' said Janet. 'Porky, make me a coffee. I've had it,' she sighed.

'Porky?' exclaimed Theo. 'Porky! Hey. Make me a cup, too, Porky.'

'I'll kill you, sister,' said David.

'He could, too,' said Theo. 'He's a killer, all right.'

'Help!' squealed Jan.

'Porky Porky Porky,' said Theo.

'You two can talk all night if you want. I'm off to bed. I'm on again come morning. Least it means I'll be home to cook you a nice dinner tomorrow night. Pork, maybe? Maybe Theo would like to come?'

'Great,' said Theo. 'Thanks. Always enjoy a meal with old Porky.'

Sunday, too, they spent together. They wandered the city and then sat in the sun on the wharves happy in the company of each other.

'Go and see Gretel when you get home,' said Theo.

'Dunno,' said David. 'I don't think I want to.'

'I think you should. Think about it. Not too many old grandmothers would understand things like she does, even if you do think she's got it all wrong. Please go and see her. She does think you're someone special. Like a helluva lot more special than she thinks I am. And I will be down again. I will. Soon.'

'Yeah,' said David.

Theo lit a cigarette. 'Face it, kid. You've done a helluva lot for me, but you still gotta stop me smoking.'

'You reckon I could? Just keep running. Probably counteracts something. Anyway, when I think of things, I don't think I've done all that much for you. Caused you pain? A lot, eh?' David looked away.

'You'll never know,' said Theo. 'We better get to your

114

sister's and give her a hand.'

'Why?'

'Come off it, Porky. She's worked all day and now she's getting a feed for the two of us? Be fair.'

David jumped up and laughed. 'Yeah. Right. After all, was me you called goody football boots. Just don't give yourself no halo. You still gotta tidy up that tip of a house of yours before your old lady gets back. Come on.'

He was alone with his sister. Theo had eaten, stayed and then gone. David made cocoa for the two of them and they sat together on the sofa. 'Good weekend, Porks?'

'The best,' he said, and got down on his knees in front of her. 'Please please please please please don't call me that in front of anyone. Please. Promise?'

'Nope,' she said. 'Old habits die too hard. Wasn't it great you met up with Theo in town?' She looked at him.

'Yeah.'

'Nice guy. Can't see him fitting in too good down home.'

'He was okay.'

'Bit rich for the countryside, I'd say,' said Janet.

'No. He was all right.'

They sat still, quiet for a few moments. 'Come on. Drink that up. Got to get you away in the morning. Come on,' Janet urged.

'Janet,' he said.

'Yes?'

'Have you ever been in love with someone?'

'Why? Why do you ask?'

'Well, just have you?'

'If you must know,' she looked at him and frowned, 'Yes, I have.'

'Jan . . .?'

'Out with it,' she said.

'Can you tell me does it always hurt? Does it always hurt so really, really bad?'

'What . . .?' she began.

'Like there's nothing else but that feeling and it goes on and on and it's in your mind and things go wrong and don't work out and there's nothing, nothing you can do to make it feel better.' He looked at his sister and he breathed hard. 'Does it always have to hurt?'

As he looked at her, so she looked at him and his eyes filled, his lip trembled and he bit it hard, very hard, but it stopped nothing. It all overflowed. She held her arms open for him and he sobbed loudly, noisily, wetly. 'What . . .? Who . . .?' She held him away from her and looked into his face. David didn't speak. 'Dear God,' she murmured. 'It wasn't me you came to see at all. Oh, God, you poor poor thing.'

'How did you guess?'

'You just told me, man.'

'I didn't . . .'

'Does anybody else know?'

'His grandmother. I think it might have been that she guessed, too. There is nothing to know.'

'Mum? Dad? Of course not. God, what you're telling me is you've had no one to talk to?'

'I've had Theo to talk to and he's had me. We do talk.'

'You've got me, man. You tell me. You tell me what you want,' said Janet.

'You don't mind?' he sounded surprised.

116

'Mind? Mind? Of course I bloody mind. I mind about you. You talk to me, do you hear? You talk to me now. You talk to me whenever you want. Whenever you need. You stupid little idiot! You could've talked to Mum and Dad. They love you. So much, they love you.' She shrugged. 'Yeah. Well, guess that mightn't have worked. Dunno.' She sounded very like her brother. 'There must have been someone?'

'What? You mean the guidance guy at school?' He managed a smile.

'Don't tell me,' she said. 'It's not still old Bob Green?' She started to laugh. 'Yeah, love. That's sure a problem.'

There was a small hint of hysteria in his laugh. 'Can you hear him? Eh? "Go for a long run, men. Take a cold shower?" Only with me he'd have put in another bit: "I'll lend you me hunting knife, Davy. Cut 'em off, lad."'

Janet looked at her brother. They laughed together.

'Jan. You don't think I'm dirty, do you?'

'Do you think you're dirty, Davy?'

'No, I don't. I'm not.'

'In the long run, Davy, that's all that counts.'

'Why did it happen like this? To me?' And then he remembered. 'Or to him? To Theo?'

'I don't have those sort of answers. I don't think anyone has those sort of answers,' said Janet. 'Why does anything like this, like that, happen to any of us?'

They talked on into the night.

11

Again he walked to the Meyer house. He stood at the gate, uncertain, hesitating. Sucking in his breath and standing straighter, he walked down the drive.

The sight that hit his eyes made him gasp. Curving, sloping away from the terrace in a broad belt was a sky-blue carpet of grape hyacinth in full bloom. A richness of blue that immediately drew the eye. The blue lawn.

'I told you,' Gretel Meyer came up behind him and touched his arm. 'I know you did not believe me. I was right, eh?'

'Your blue lawn,' he whispered. 'It's so lovely.'

'It is,' she said. 'Come.' She pressed his arm and indicated that he should follow her. She led the way to the front of the house. 'There,' she said. 'And there is the other.'

Its perfume clung in the air of the little recess where it grew. The white lilac. The panicles of flower drooped from pale, new-growing greenery. It stood alone against the wall, uncluttered by any other growth.

'Yes,' he said. 'Yes.'

'Sit there.' She pointed to the stone bench. 'I'll get us a drink.' She didn't ask if he wanted one and soon she came back with a bottle of wine and two kitchen tumblers. 'I think you and me might have a toast, eh?'

'What for?' He was puzzled.

She smiled at him. 'To the white lilac? To friendship?'

They drank. While they drank they sat silently and both looked at the bush. Then he asked her, 'You did go back to it, didn't you?'

'Of course I went back.' No hesitation.

'They were gone?'

'All gone.'

'Where?'

'The camps. The gas-chambers. The ovens.' Simply. 'I did not know it all then. Later, it was later, I found out.'

'Why didn't you stay?'

'Should I have stayed?' She shrugged. 'No. There was no welcome. "Dirty Jew" I heard spoken and spat. There were those who looked, and in their eyes you could see they thought it a pity the job had not been quite finished. Hah!' The bark-laugh. 'Yes. Some said it, too.'

'They just couldn't,' he whispered. 'They couldn't say that.'

The woman drank, deeply, and ignored his comment. 'The lilac bush stood. The street, the house, the houses, all unchanged.'

'Your little leather purse?'

'A good memory.' She looked at him and smiled very slightly. 'It was there. I got it. I left.'

'Where did you go?'

'I made my way to the west. Through the Russians. It was early, yet, and the iron fist not quite in place. Things were possible, one way or another. Much, much confusion. People, thousands, hundreds of thousands, more more more, all on the move. I became a speck in the tide. Weeks into months. I do not know. It was as if I was numb. Memory? The bits and pieces? Some fit, some don't . . .'

'Was there no help?' he asked.

'If there was, I don't remember. A madhouse. Help? I suppose there must have been some. After all,' she shrugged again, 'I am here. I am alive to this day. Food? Somewhere to sleep for a night, for some nights . . . food, yes. Clothing? Simply, I moved westward but I don't think, I am sure I don't truly know why. Soldiers. The armies of the east and the west. British. American. The Red Army. Sometimes both and others, too.

'Slowly, so slowly I am back to some sort of life. Slowly, so slowly I start to wonder where the tide might take me. Slowly it became of some importance where that tide might wash me up. I looked. I listened. I learnt.'

'How old were you then?' David asked.

'Old?' She looked at him. 'You read your Bible? I was as old as Methuselah. Older than you could ever imagine. Old? Hah! In all truth, my dear, I was younger than you are now, as you sit there in front of me so very very concerned about the long long ago.

'A town. Some town. I don't know where. Towards Austria. Maybe Austria. Boundaries came, boundaries went. I sheltered. Two, three others with me. Three, four women, ragged, hungry, pathetic. And drunk, drunken Russian soldiers. They drank and they yelled, those warriors. They see us. There is no escape for the flotsam, jetsam women. I see him now, the one who took me. As young as I and as scared, no doubt. As scared? Hah! Worse things than him had scared me. What does it matter? Five minutes, ten, no more. There had been much worse. Soon it was over and they went.

Yet, yet, I remember . . . So scared, this baby warrior, this little conqueror, conquering Slav of the steppes or wherever. All I see of him, now, are his eyes, the eyes of a drunk-bold swaggering boy. I see them today. You know where? In the face of my grandson, Theodore.' Gretel Meyer drank the rest of her wine.

'And you came here?'

She relaxed, poured more wine for the two of them. 'You must come back for that part of the journey. The hops, the steps, the jumps. The chances and, what you say, the flukes? Some years, it took. Yes, we came here. The two of us.' She looked at David. 'Theo's mother, my daughter, and myself.'

'Things got better?'

'We survived. One way or another we survived.' She spoke the words without the slightest trace of bitterness. Then she stood. 'Face it, kid, as my grandson would say. They couldn't have got much worse,' she laughed.

David stood, too. 'Thank you for telling me your story. If you want to, sometime, I would like to know about the hops and the steps and the jumps. Does Theo know it?'

'Theo?' She smiled at him. 'Of course he does. It is his story, too. Come, boy. I shall walk to the gate with you.'

It was at the gate that he said, 'Gretel. I've got to say I'm sorry for what I said to you when Theo went away.'

'I did what I thought was best,' said Gretel Meyer. 'It seemed best at the time. I was not certain whether it was right or whether it was necessary. I thought of Theo, and of his mother. I thought of you, David, and of your parents. Maybe, I don't know, I should have trusted a little more. Who knows?'

'I've seen Theo,' he said.

'I'm glad,' she said, but did not question further.

'We won't lose touch with each other,' said David.

'No,' she said. 'I think maybe you won't and I am glad. At times there seems little warmth in this world for any of us.' She shivered slightly. 'Off you go now.' She touched his arm.

He looked back into the garden behind her. 'Sure is one beautiful blue lawn,' said David.

'I told you it would be,' said Gretel. 'I told you it would be. The blue lawn.'